T0149443

LIFE
FRAGMENTS

BETTE CYZNER

iUniverse LLC
Bloomington

LIFE FRAGMENTS

iUniverse books may be ordered through booksellers or by contacting:

iUniverse LLC
1663 Liberty Drive
Bloomington, IN 47403
www.iuniverse.com
1-800-Authors (1-800-288-4677)

Because of the dynamic nature of the Internet, any web addresses or links contained in this book may have changed since publication and may no longer be valid. The views expressed in this work are solely those of the author and do not necessarily reflect the views of the publisher, and the publisher hereby disclaims any responsibility for them.

Any people depicted in stock imagery provided by Thinkstock are models, and such images are being used for illustrative purposes only. Certain stock imagery © Thinkstock.

ISBN: 978-1-4917-2414-9 (sc)
ISBN: 978-1-4917-2415-6 (e)

Printed in the United States of America.

iUniverse rev. date: 02/12/2014

WITH GRATITUDE TO . . .

.The One Above Who allowed me to reach this day

.My husband Abe for emotional and technical support

.My knowledgeable and conscientious editor, Theresa Riccardi

.The UFT's Creative Writing course, my instructor Muriel Bart, and to my wonderful classmates, especially Frances Taormina, for their insights and guidance.

MORNING STAR

After the night has nearly passed,
At the time that the heavenly displays
Are melting into the brightening skies,
The morning star, with silvery splendor
Shines brighter, stronger than all of the rest.
Just as the concluding days of my life
Are blessed when I put pen to paper.
My imaginings, so long earth-bound
Finally freed, soar heavenward,
My hidden passion at last given life.

FRAGMENTS

Later in her life she often sported dark glasses and a cap that obscured much of her physiognomy. Many people, she realized, had no idea what she really looked like. That pleased her.

The friends and family who attended her funeral brought their own recollections of relationships with her, each comprising a tiny kaleidoscopic portion of the puzzle of her life. Even combined, the pieces would never have been capable of conveying the entire picture of this woman. How could they? The lynchpin of hidden but crucial events was missing, and without this understanding, the shards would not adhere one to another.

Thus, as she would have wished, she essentially remained a mystery— so much so that few were even aware of just how much of an enigma she had actually been. To someone whose unstated theme song had been Melissa Manchester's "Don't Cry Out Loud," who identified with stuffed animals that had enduring grins indelibly etched on their faces even as they were pulled apart by destructive children, that fact would have been very satisfying.

FRAGMENTS
OF THE
HOLOCAUST

THE SHLEMAZAL

The shlemiel spills the soup on the shlemazal.
—Yiddish joke

"A *groisser shlemazal!*"—a terrible unfortunate—*neboh!* (pity) was the consensus. The subject of such pity and derision in the small Russian stetl (village) Imnovitch in 1920? Mendel, of course; Mendel Moskowitz, eighteen years old, an apprentice tailor, and already a loser.

He had inherited none of his drunken father's good looks, or his mother's skill with the needle, which in her hands, seemed to fly, leaving almost invisible but uncannily strong stitches. Despite her toil, the large family was desperately poor. Many mealtimes, only the aroma of groats or potatoes (and not in such plentiful supply, either) permeated the dirt-floored hut, the wooden shack itself seeming to shiver in the frigid Ukrainian wind.

It would be a kindness to say that as a child in *cheder* (Hebrew school), Mendel had not been one of the more outstanding students. He had earned more than his share of slaps and kicks from the impatient teachers. Even when the source of annoyance stemmed from other boys, somehow it was Mendel's hand or head that would intercept the blows that had been destined for the perpetrators.

Circumstances had been about the same in public school, so that when he dropped out at the age of eleven to begin to learn the tailoring trade, the educational system did not exactly go into mourning. In fact, most of the teachers were just as glad. "One less Jew," they snorted derisively.

Outside the halls of learning, Mendel's bad luck continued to dog him. Inevitably, when the heavy-hoofed horses pulled wagons through the town's narrow, unpaved streets, it would be Mendel who was covered with thick brown mud, while other pedestrians would suffer only tiny, light splatters.

As you can imagine, the *shadchante* (matchmaker) was not tripping over her long skirts in her haste to match Mendel up. The choices that were offered to Mrs. Moskowitz for her son—a severely retarded girl, a shrewish thirty-year-old widow—were so unpalatable that Mendel had no hesitancy about voicing his rejection. The *shadchante* had tossed her bewigged head with annoyance when Mendel's mother informed her of her son's distaste for the proposed candidates. "What do you want, a princess for such a *shlemazal?*" she shouted, curling her lip in disgust.

Had anyone bothered to look more closely, they would have seen, from time to time, an uncharacteristically calculating look flit over Mendel's face as his narrow brown eyes became even narrower. Mendel had a plan. Then, once again, his curly black head would bend over to continue his unremarkable tailoring.

When he had scrimped and saved enough of his meager wages, he purchased a ticket, kissed his parents and siblings farewell, and departed for America.

The journey was terrible—two weeks in airless steerage. Even though it was the middle of June, and not traditionally a tumultuous month on the North Atlantic, waves bounced the small ship about, in the manner of a toy boat in a rapidly filling bathtub. Had the crew known about Mendel's penchant for ill fortune, they might have tossed him overboard, like a modern-day Jonah. In Biblical times and in the twentieth century, no one wanted a *shlemazal* on board.

As it was, they made it, all vomitously ill, to New York Harbor. In the crowded and noisy immigration hall, Mendel was held for several hours by health authorities. It was finally determined that the red lesions on the left side of his face were a result of the ship's rough planks scratching Mendel's head as he slept on the floor, and were not caused by some contagious skin disease.

By the time he was released into his new country, all of his "*shiff breeder*" (ship brethren) had dispersed, any assistance that they might have extended departing right along with them.

Mendel spent the first two nights in his new country sleeping in a park, being soaked by heavy summer showers.

On the third day, Mendel, ravenously hungry and exuding a repulsive stale odor, stumbled into a Lower East Side bakery to plead for some food. He had never begged in his life. "I had to wait to come to the golden land to become a *kaptsan* (beggar)?" he thought sadly. "I'm such a *shlemazal!*"

With great effort, Mendel pulled open the bakery's heavy wooden door. Air, redolent with tantalizing sugary-vanilla fragrances, rose up to meet him. In Europe, he had been hungry many times, but he had never starved, not like this. His stomach was contracting painfully with the lack of food, and vital pounds had already been melted off his narrow, slender frame due to his involuntary fast.

Sarah, the plump, gray-haired owner, had compassion on the beaten-down, dirty *rachmonos* (pity) case that had just lurched into her establishment. Quickly, she fed him fresh warm rolls and hot, strong coffee, which Mendel gratefully wolfed down. Then Sarah presented him with an even greater gift—directions to a settlement house, and to a woman there who, she assured Mendel, could be of help, "Maybe even to such a *shlemazal*," Sarah thought to herself.

Theoretically, Feige Steinberg did not seem to be someone who would be the object of sympathetic clucking and sad shakes of the head. A trained social worker, she had graduated from Hunter College with high honors. She held a responsible job that garnered great respect. Her name meant "Birdie," but the only avian vision that she conjured up was that of a sharp-beaked vulture. Her nose had more bumps and twists than a *Shabbos* challah bread, and her thin, mouse-brown hair hung in stringy wisps. Feige viewed the world through thick, rimless glasses that served to obscure the brightness of her intelligent brown eyes.

Although Feige presented a generally slender appearance, her body's fat had collected exclusively from her waist to her thighs, flaring out unflatteringly like a ballerina's tutu. This unfortunate conspiracy of her face and figure resulted in the creation of a real *meeskeit* (ugly one). Feige loved children, but now, at age twenty-five, she had sadly come to accept the fact that she would probably never marry and have a family. Instead, her great love and dedication was channeled towards her settlement house clientele. But the day that Mendel shlepped himself into her office, she realized that she had not been faced with the task of helping such a *shlemazal* for quite some time. However, only slightly daunted, and like a homely guardian angel, she began to work her magic.

5

She sent Mendel to the public bathhouse, giving him clean, used shirts and slacks which had been stored in her office closet for just such a purpose. Feige managed, even on such short notice, to provide him with sleeping space on the floor of a stuffy, crowded tenement room. The conditions in the apartment were only marginally better than on Mendel's sea voyage. The sole improvement over the miserable passage in steerage was the building's immobility. Mendel also received a small allowance for the purchase of food.

Finding employment for her newest "project," Feige realized, would prove difficult.

"I'm sorry," she told Mendel in her American-accented Yiddish. "There are no jobs for *shneiders* (tailors) right now. The factories are full."

Mendel slumped with dejection. He had hoped for a new start in his new land. Had his misfortune, like a wailing seabird, flown over his ship to arrive with him in America?

"Well, there is one position available," Feige offered, shuffling some papers on her rickety "schoolteacher's" desk, and then raising her head to look at her newest social service client, "but you might not want it."

"Anything, I'll take anything," Mendel begged, although he had a mental picture of having to clean up after some large, well-fed horses—a job for a *shlemazal*.

"Take the address; it's right around the corner on Broome Street. They need an assistant badly."

The establishment so desperately in need of help was Goldstein's Funeral Home.

At first, Mendel found the work difficult, but he steeled himself with the thoughts that he was, at least, earning a steady salary and that, unlike so many other newcomers, he was not forced to desecrate the holy Sabbath by working on it. It was also reassuring to know that regardless of economic conditions, there would always be a need for his services.

The job became less stressful when he forced himself to stop noting the resemblance of his waxy subjects to friends and neighbors in Imnovitch. He began to take comfort in the psalms that were recited as the bodies were ritually prepared for burial.

Through the next few years, Mendel's living standard improved only slightly.

When other young men invited him to join them at a social club or dance, he declined. Once again Mendel was saving his meager wages. He only left his room to go to work, shop for necessities, go to *shul* (synagogue), or from time to time, to apprise Feige of his progress.

Over the months and years, their friendship blossomed as they learned to ignore one another's superficial imperfections and to focus on the kind hearts that lay below the surfaces, like nuggets of gold beneath turbid streams.

As his small secret *peckel* (bundle) of savings grew—he didn't trust banks—one more destination was added to Mendel's short itinerary—the noisy, crowded shipping office. There, Mendel incrementally purchased tickets for his Imnovitch family to come to the New World.

Gradually, even through difficult economic times, Mendel's sisters Rachel, Esther, and Beila, and their families were able, with Feige's help, to become part of the fabric of the Lower East Side. Sadly, his older sister Miriam, to whom Mendel had been the closest, had died in childbirth, the baby ripping at her insides like a Cossack's sword. Her bereaved husband, the rather well-to-do Leibel, had immediately severed ties with his late wife's family. "Perhaps he wouldn't have been so hasty, if we had been wealthy or renowned scholars? Maybe if I wasn't such a *shlemazal?*" Mendel had mentally flagellated himself mournfully.

Mendel's mother had also made the voyage to New York. His father had died years before, when, in a drunken stupor, he had gone to sleep at midnight in the center of one of Imnovitch's larger streets. A fully loaded wagon, racing to market day in Nezhin, three towns away, had run over him in the frigid pre-dawn darkness.

For the first time ever, Mendel's heart swelled with pride when he realized that it had been due to his initiative that so many of his family members lived in the *"goldeneh medina"* (the golden land), the United States.

He was also gratified when his clientele expressed their appreciation for his kindness through their difficult time of loss. Empathy came easily to the life-long *shlemazal*. Mendel's storied compassion attracted an ever-increasing number of bereaved new Americans to Goldstein's.

As the old Yiddish proverb reminds us, "Even a broken clock is right twice a day."

Mendel's brother Yankel resembled their father, both in his handsome appearance and in his love for alcohol. Yankel had refused Mendel's offer of immigration, perhaps because he feared that new circumstances might prove an obstacle to his pursuit of the fruit of the vine, or possibly because he was so anaesthetized by liquor that he really didn't care about his future, or the future of his growing family.

However, Devaira, Yankel's kind, long-suffering wife, had other ideas. She herself had a fragile, skeletal appearance and a chronic, hacking cough. Even if she was to attempt the horrendous voyage, she understood that she and her four young children would probably be sent back to Europe faster than Yankel could finish a bottle of whiskey

But there was Tseral.

Devaira wrote to Mendel in her semi-literate, spiky hand. She begged him to send for her sweet and bright eleven-year—old daughter. In America, Devaira knew, Tseral could have a life. Right after *Pesach* (Passover) of 1939, the ticket arrived.

"You're sending her to Mendel, to that *shlemazal?*" The townspeople asked incredulously.

Even though it was nearly twenty years since Mendel had left, his reputation for ill fortune continued. Instances of his bad luck survived in folk tales of sorts, even though most of these events had never actually transpired.

. . ."And then the frightened horse started running wildly, and Mendel was still on him!"

. . ."The wagon crashed into the house, and part of the wall collapsed. Guess who had just gone in to deliver some clothes, and guess who that wall fell on?"

. . ."The rain had washed away part of the street, but you couldn't see the hole, because it was covered by water and mud. Of course, wouldn't you know, Mendel, carrying a challah for *Shabbos,* was the first to walk there and fall down into that mess!"

After 1933, when Germany elected the crazy little man with the mustache who seemed to be making trouble for the Jews there, the Mendel jokes took on a political aspect.

. . ."Mendel felt too sick to stay on the boat to America, so he got off—in Hamburg!"

Devaira stuck out her bony chin defiantly.

"Mendel's not a *shlemazal* now! He's married to Feige, an American social worker, and he's a partner in a funeral business."

"If Mendel's in the funeral business . . ." began wealthy David Blumberg, his heavy-set frame doubling over with the impetus of his mirth. He was chuckling so hard that he had trouble articulating his punch line, "If Mendel's in the funeral business," he repeated, sputtering, "people in America will stop dying!"

He tossed back his head as he emitted boisterous chortles, arrogant in his perceived cleverness and good fortune.

The townspeople's laughter was so loud as it blended in with Blumberg's guffaws that it drifted even over the highest rooftops of Imnovitch, and drowned out Devaira's thin voice.

With horrifying prescience, she exclaimed, "She's going, no matter what you say. At least I can save Tseral!"

Tseral left at the beginning of June, traveling with Devaira's cousins from Nezhin and their three young children. Throughout the long but smooth voyage, Tseral happily tended to the youngsters. She was still fussing over them when Mendel and Feige came to collect her at Ellis Island, but she was also ready for the golden future that awaited her in the golden land.

With Feige's loving encouragement, Tseral mastered English and managed, over the years, to graduate from both Julia Richman High School and Hunter College with high honors.

In medical school the beautiful Tseral (now Shirley), met fellow student Ben Eisenberg, whom she later married. The young couple and their four children would love and honor Feige and Mendel as cherished parents and grandparents for the remainder of the supposedly "luckless" couple's long lives.

Not long after Tseral's June departure from Imnovitch, the "Mendel the *Shlemazal*" jokes began to fade away, like the summer swallows that depart Russia as cooler weather begins to approach.

There were much more urgent concerns after Germany had marched into Poland in the bloody September of 1939. Fear, especially amongst the Jews, swept quickly eastward to the Ukrainian villages and towns.

Less than two years later, the Nazis rolled into Imnovitch. The Jews of the town were forced to the outskirts and ordered to dig ditches. The loud sounds that were heard over the rooftops this time, instead of laughter, were sharp German commands, terrified screams, and staccato shots, for when the excavations they were forced to dig were completed, the town's Jewish men, women, and children were machine-gunned into the waiting trenches. No Jew who had remained in Imnovitch managed to survive.

If anyone *had* lived, they might have finally understood that just as Heaven veils the names of the thirty-six *Tsadikkim,*˙ it often obscures the identities of those who are loved by the Creator for their kind hearts, and are chosen to receive the ultimate of blessings and luck.

---

* *According to legend, the righteous persons in whose merit the world is permitted to continue to exist.*

HOLOCAUST NIGHTMARES

Survivor, urbane and jovial in the light of day,
Tortured victim through the ebony night.
Bed sheets molded to trembling body
By perspiration, twists, and spasms.
His mournful wails and shrill, loud keening,
Piercing the darkness as bullets penetrate flesh.
Vivid images of hangings and shootings
Crematorium fires bridging past and present
Torn memories of murdered family and friends
Permitting no rest, no peaceful slumber.
Days of terror, relived nocturnally.
Survivor, unsure in which dimension
His life and reality exist.

SHPRINZA

Fifty-five degrees—a record low for April twenty-fourth in Miami
Beach!

Joggers, their jerseys zipped to the top, greeted each other with calls
of "Cold!" as they hugged themselves in the unseasonable early morning
chill. The sun's warming rays, which would have mitigated the unusual
coolness, were hidden behind smokepuff-like clouds in the slate gray sky.
Waves of teal green crashed to the shore, their foam like lacy veils agitated
by the wind.

On other, more pleasant mornings that, unlike today, were the norm
for this time of year, I was always attracted to the boardwalk—not only
for the purpose of burning off some of the calories contained in our
hotel's delicious and bounteous meals, but also to admire the beautiful
vistas that its meandering path revealed, and to be refreshed by gentle
breezes redolent with the salty smell of the ocean.

On the beach side of the promenade lay three distinct bands of
color—green scrub, then the beige of the sand where footsteps had
created indentations with darker shadings, and finally the gray-blue of
the water. On the side of the boardwalk closest to the hotels were green,
manicured lawns with turquoise pools, white lounge chairs, and inviting
umbrellas in rainbow colors. Towering, carefully cultivated palm trees
were closely encircled by flowers in hues of red and pink.

But this day my walk was motivated by a desire to be alone with my
thoughts, bitter and tear-inducing as the *maror* (bitter herbs, a reminder
of the bitterness of the Jews' slavery in Egypt) that we had eaten at last
night's Passover *seder* (meal).

I passed the Seville Hotel where my friend Hilde and her husband
had vacationed and proudly logged miles on their pedometers. My hike
took me farther south, near the Roney Plaza. Here my wealthy cousin had
rented "for the season" and my best friend's artistic mother had created
a mural on her own terrace. Where the beach curved to the left, past the

boardwalk's end, I could see the pink exterior of The Shelbourne Hotel. My aunt had been a guest there, but not even the Miami sun could warm her back to health. The one comfort amidst these melancholy musings was that at least these people, now all deceased, had enjoyed more or less normal life spans.

Unlike Shprinza, my husband's oldest sister.

Shprinza was born in Chrzanow, Poland, in the 1920s. She lived the life of a typical Polish-Jewish girl, involved with school, friends, and even a trip to the fascinating Vyelichke Mines, which featured green underground lakes and figures carved out of salt.

In September of 1939, her father was killed as the Germans invaded, and what was to remain of her life changed dramatically. She suffered through ghettoization, hunger and fear, and the deportation of her mother. Finally, in 1942, she herself was sent to Auschwitz. She did not survive. Shprinza was about sixteen when she was committed to the gas, to the flames, a beautiful flower that had just begun to bloom, one of six million dead.

My thoughts drifted back to last Passover. At that time, we had stayed at the same lovely hotel that we were currently visiting. During religious services, I was seated near a mature woman in the ladies' section. Afterward, I pointed her out to my husband.

"You know, that lady is smaller and blonder, but I think that if your sister had survived, that's how she might have looked."

My mind was haunted by the image of a middy-bloused teenager in a group photo from her school—the only photo of Shprinza that we had. This woman had the same head of curly hair, full lips, prominent cheekbones, fine nose, and modestly downcast eyes. She was about the age that Shprinza would have been had she lived.

My husband shrugged. Although he studied portraiture, it was too painful to use his skills to make such a comparison.

The woman had slowly faded from my consciousness after the holiday's end.

Time quickly raced by. Now Passover had once again arrived and we returned to our Miami Beach hotel. As was the custom before the seders, most ladies waited outside the synagogue while the men completed the evening prayers. I found myself seated next to the woman who had reminded me so strongly of Shprinza the previous year, and we began to chat.

She told me her father had had the foresight to leave Vienna in the 1930s, before the Nazi annexation. The entire family had immigrated to the United States. She was now a widow, but she lived on Long Island, near her daughter, son-in-law, and grandchildren. She belonged to a gym and took interesting courses.

A life that could have been Shprinza's in another time, another place.

"I'm Bette," I said, putting out my hand.

"I'm Jenny," the woman smiled, and once again I noted the resemblance to Shprinza.

"Oh, you have a popular name, now that there are so many Jennifers, and famous ones, too!" I laughed.

"Well, I always liked my name," she replied. "But my Yiddish name, now that's another matter."

"Really?" I queried.

"When I first heard it, I didn't know whether to laugh or to cry. I wanted to laugh because I thought it was so ugly, but I wanted to cry because it was mine!"

She waved her hand in a downward gesture, as if dismissing the undesirable name.

"And what is it?" I asked, looking at her expectantly.

"Ah, you've probably never heard it; it's very unusual."

"Really? Try me," I smiled.

"It's Shprinza."

"*WHAT did you say?*" I leaned forward, not believing my ears.

"See, I told you that you wouldn't have heard of it."

"No, no, that's not the reason . . ."

"Hi, Mom, come on, we have to start the seder!"

Jenny's daughter stood in front of us, beaming. Her black silk suit rustled as she bent to kiss her mother. The sweet, heavy fragrance of her perfume filled the air.

"Good *Yontiff* (Happy Holiday)," they both wished me. Jenny slowly rose, leaning on her daughter's extended hands.

"Good *Yontiff*," I barely squeaked out. I was trembling violently.

Soon my husband emerged from the synagogue. I pulled him to one side of the brightly lit marble lobby that was now buzzing with festive conversations.

After I told him of my evening's discovery, we were both shaking. We slowly walked into the beautifully decorated dining room to celebrate Passover, the festival of freedom. In Jewish tradition, hard-boiled eggs signify mourning. It was particularly poignant that the rabbi mentioned these were on the seder table to commemorate those who had died in Egyptian slavery, who did not live to see liberation, just as Shprinza had not survived so many centuries later.

That night, neither my husband nor I got much sleep.

On the morning after that heart-rending revelation, in the chilly gray light, I joined the early-morning joggers as their footfalls echoed on the brown boardwalk. Water from the previous night's rain had pooled into tiny puddles—a subtle warning that certain areas could prove slippery.

And now it appeared that the foam on the waves was not a lacy veil at all, but instead a wispy shroud. I looked at the beige sand with its darker shadings, and I wondered how much beach would be required to contain six million footsteps. I also pondered if, on this holiday of family closeness, a ghostly presence had reached out through an amazing coincidence to reaffirm the eternity of that bond.

A strong wind rose up over the water just then, and bore droplets inland to the boardwalk, but the ocean was not the source of the moisture that stung my eyes.

Shopping For Justice—
The Final Witness

The early October air felt crisp and invigorating. Amber patches of sunlight fell on the concrete underneath the department store's façade, but it was still chilly at 9:53 a.m.

Rachel Weiss Ginsberg was glad that she had arrived early. She was one of the very first customers on line waiting for Alexander's to open at ten o'clock. Although this store always offered good values, Columbus Day sales were special. Shoppers of all ages, sizes, races, and sexes were excitedly waving newspaper ads that pictured the items that they anticipated "getting a great deal on."

No one in the waiting crowd gave Rachel a second glance. She was petite, with curly dark hair, and could have been taken for Spanish, Italian, or the Polish Jewess that she was. Her eyes, had they not seen horrendous suffering, might have been vivacious and flashing. Now they were merely responsive and intelligent.

Rachel noticed that many in the crowd were checking their watches, shaking their heads with annoyance.

"It's after ten already!" a mature blonde woman grumbled, pointing to a 'fast" brown clock that was situated over a shoe store, on the other side of congested Sixty-Third Drive.

These people were so spoiled! Rachel reflected bitterly. They couldn't know what it meant to be unable to express impatience and outrage with real misery!

Through rain, snow, biting wind and freezing temperature, she and her fellow prisoners had been forced to stand for hours on the *Appelplatz*** clad only in thin striped dresses and wood or fabric shoes. When it suited the thermally dressed Nazis, the prisoners were finally permitted to go to

---

** *Assembly point in the concentration camp where prisoners were counted.*

their backbreaking jobs as slave laborers, manufacturing supplies for the German army. At the end of the ten-plus-hour day, the inmates *might* be given watery soup and sawdust-y bread. If they were lucky.

Rachel tried to mentally push the images of her past away. She was here in America, in Forest Hills, free, ready to shop for some "special purchase" jewel-toned sweaters to delight her daughters. She planned to store them in anticipation of the upcoming Chanukah holiday, two months away.

For many years, Rachel had been unable to afford to buy more than the basics. Even now, when she was financially secure, the habit of frugality had been deeply ingrained, and "retail therapy" was, to her, a strange concept.

In contrast, frequenting stores appeared to be an avocation, a leisure activity central to the lives of many of the American mothers of the friends of Rachel's children. This perceived frivolity was just one more reason for the feeling of many survivors that anyone fortunate enough to be U.S.-born, those who hadn't suffered through the concentration camps, couldn't possibly empathize with their pain. How could these lucky, unscarred Americans comprehend that, even at a festive occasion, faces of beloved murdered relatives would suddenly rise up to replace the elegantly tuxedoed and gowned guests. Rather than risk being misunderstood, the survivors formed a tight, insular group—a subculture within the Jewish community.

While they had still been in the Displaced Persons' Camp, Rachel, the only member of the once-large Weiss family who hadn't been annihilated by the Nazis, had married Isaac Ginsberg, a tall blond survivor from Krakow. When they arrived in Brooklyn in 1950, Mindel (Mindy), now a married teacher herself, was three, and Esti (Esther), a physical therapist, had been an infant. Shlomo (Steven), presently a pre-veterinary student, was born in 1954.

Each child had been named for a greatly missed family member who had been murdered, but as Rachel, bowing her head in sadness, had observed many times, she would have had to have given birth to hundreds of babies to honor the memories of all those on both sides of the family who had been wiped out.

The couple had worked very hard in the years after settling in the United States. Isaac had toiled in a handbag factory by day and, slumped with fatigue, attended evening school to learn English and accounting. Rachel labored as a neighborhood seamstress while caring for her growing family.

Eventually, Isaac had been able to pass his C.P.A. exam, and currently had three accountants working for him. It had been many years since Rachel had sewn for pay, and now she rarely even stitched outfits for herself or her girls—ready-made was more convenient and, many times, actually cost less.

Her own wardrobe consisted of subdued hues—never vibrant or even bright. Such colors, Rachel believed, conveyed an air of cheer, and a carefree attitude with which she just couldn't identify.

Not long now until the store's opening time. Rachel turned around to survey the ever-growing crowd on the line behind her. Oh, they were there all right, shifting in place with anticipation, heads bobbing to obtain a better view of the still-closed doors. Suddenly Rachel froze.

It would not have been easy to miss her; her broad five-foot-ten frame towered over most of the shoppers. The thin blond hair, even with a "curly" permanent, still hung limply, and the square jaw and pointed chin still jutted out defiantly under frosty blue eyes.

After all these years, could it really be Irma Steinbrecher, the incredibly merciless guard at the Polish concentration camp where Rachel had been imprisoned?

Rachel felt herself begin to tremble violently with fear and hatred as her heart pounded loudly. She experienced a sudden chill, and quickly closed the buttons of her gray sweater. She forced herself to calm down and commenced taking deep breaths of the cool air.

Perhaps she was wrong. Had her earlier thoughts possibly colored her perceptions? How in the world could she be certain?

Before the war, the red-headed Feldman sisters had lived a few blocks away from Rachel Weiss in Warsaw. The girls would greet her in the street, but because they were respectively two and three years older than Rachel, the teenagers had never really socialized with her.

By 1943, in the camp, such age differences ceased to matter; one shaven-headed skeleton was much like another. It was, in fact, amazing that they had even recognized each other in the freezing, cement-floored uniform factory. From that time, they had attempted to stay close.

On that overcast, cold morning at roll call (the Nazis always checked attendance at least twice a day to ensure that no prisoner had escaped), the sisters were standing next to fifteen-year-old Rachel when Steinbrecher spied Blima, the younger girl, swaying with fatigue and illness. Sarah, her older sibling, was desperately attempting to support her.

"Stand up by yourself, Jewish whore!" the guard had thundered. In contrast to the shivering prisoners' thin uniforms, Steinbrecher was dressed in a long khaki wool coat topped by a warm brown knit hat and leather gloves. Blima struggled to right herself, but she was too weak and cold to draw herself up. She helplessly keeled forward, slightly brushing against Steinbrecher's solid mass.

"Push into me, will you, Jew bitch? I'll teach you!" she screamed, raising her truncheon, bringing it down and down again, even after Blima fell and was writhing on the frozen ground, even after the skin that was stretched like parchment over the protruding bones had yielded up its meager blood supply. Blima's flimsy black and white inmate's dress was stained in ever-growing crimson blobs. Blood gurgled out of the young girl's mouth, and she gasped out the "*Shema*" (last prayer before death) through crimson bubbles.

Sarah, who along with the other prisoners had been transfixed with horror, emerged from her shocked state to look down at the corpse of her little sister. With a movement so quick that even Steinbrecher was caught unaware, she grabbed the guard's left hand, the hand that was closest to her, and bit as hard as she could into the back.

Steinbrecher, doubling over, howled with pain. Her yells brought two other large Nazi women running to her aid.

Rachel would never forget what happened next.

"I'm taking this *untermensch* (subhuman), this whore, this bitch, and putting her right into the oven! Gas is too good for her! Let her burn alive!" Steinbrecher bellowed.

How much could an eighty-pound scarecrow resist? The enraged guard dragged Sarah away, beating her with the truncheon that had killed her sister. Although the crematoriums were located some distance away, the prisoners could hear Sarah's screams for several minutes.

Many years later, in her sleep, Rachel still heard them.

The clanging bell announced the ten o'clock opening of Alexander's. The crowd began to surge forward.

Rachel permitted several people to go ahead of her, until she managed to step behind the strapping blonde. The door that their line fed into opened out, and the woman raised her left arm high to keep it from closing. As she planted her hand on the door frame, Rachel glimpsed a faint, curved scar like a colorless crescent moon on the back.

Sarah's "brand" had identified her murderess.

All thoughts of Chanukah sweaters were now gone. Rachel, trembling violently, followed the former guard through the store to the plus-size area, on the right, just in front of ladies' coats. Blouses in bright colors were displayed on several of the white enamel tables. Steinbrecher held up a few in rapid succession, but then put them down. Apparently, she had found none to her liking. She proceeded down the slow-moving escalator to the men's department. Rachel kept a discreet distance. Even though the store's temperature was increasing almost by the minute from the body heat of the myriad shoppers, Rachel felt as if the blood in her veins had frozen. Chills coursed up her spine.

Steinbrecher stopped once again, this time at a table that featured men's flannel work shirts. She rummaged through the stacks, and then bent to check the drawers underneath the display—the mark of a savvy Alexander's shopper.

"She must visit this store fairly often," Rachel thought to herself. Perhaps the guard's German frugality overrode the concern that she might be recognized by one of the many Jewish shoppers or, more likely, she assumed that no one who could identify her had survived.

Finally, the woman held up her prize—an ugly gray shirt that seemed incongruously skimpy. Rachel, taking shallow breaths, pretended to examine some socks. She then moved on to some neatly folded black and purple windbreakers.

Steinbrecher was on a swiftly moving check-out line—there was always extra help on sale days—and now the cashier was handing her the brown and navy paper bag with the Alexander's logo.

"Thank you," the guard said politely, but the sound of her deep, guttural voice, unchanged despite the years, sent Rachel's mind reeling. She remembered that voice yelling, cursing, decreeing death. Rachel once again began to shake uncontrollably. Her almost irresistible impulse was to shove, punch, and kick at the Nazi woman, but she realized, even in her distraught state, that such an attack would be extremely counter-productive. The guard was at least twice her size. Rachel would probably be injured, arrested, and regarded as a pitiable "nut case" whose mind had belatedly snapped after the years of hell.

A confrontation would also alert Steinbrecher that, after all, there was at least one living witness to her crimes, and she might flee without receiving any punishment. In memory of the victims, then, it was imperative that Rachel keep her emotions in check. She closed her eyes for just a moment, and took several deep breaths.

"Calm down," she cautioned herself.

Steinbrecher walked briskly through the accessories department and into ladies' loungewear, Rachel following at a discreet distance. The guard stopped to touch a pink-flowered robe, but almost immediately thrust it away. Rachel could see her mouth the words, "*schlecte qualitaet, billiges zeug*" (poor quality, junk), as she shook her head, and continued to the white and turquoise "up" escalator. Rachel, her heart still slamming against her ribs, also mounted it, several steps behind Steinbrecher.

It was as though the woman had disappeared into thin air, thought a dismayed Rachel as she reached the top landing. Rachel's eyes darted everywhere, searching, searching. No, wait! The blond head appeared through the spaces between shoppers, like a tour guide's flag.

Steinbrecher was leaving Alexander's. She exited through the side doors, and started to cross Queens Boulevard.

Rachel followed, nearly running across the broad, twelve-lane artery, to reach the other side before the light changed. Many pedestrians had been killed here because they hadn't moved swiftly enough to beat the insufficiently timed signals.

Steinbrecher casually walked to the bus stop, which was situated on 63rd Drive, about half a block off Queens Boulevard. There were several people already on the line.

Two buses picked up passengers here. One went to Rockaway, and the other headed to Greenpoint, via Glendale and Maspeth. Which would the guard take?

Rachel decided that joining the queue would seem a bit too obvious, but passing traffic could clearly be seen through the glass doors of McCrory's Five and Ten Cents Store. She walked hastily inside and turned to face the street as she fished change from her brown shoulder bag, only stepping briefly away from her post in response to shoppers' mutterings of "excuse me," and "pardon me," as they entered and exited.

After about ten minutes, an ancient orange and beige bus lumbered up, brakes groaning. The black and white sign on the front announced its destination—Greenpoint. Steinbrecher was already moving toward the front door. She mounted the steps, her broad body leaning heavily on the railing.

Rachel quickly left McCrory's, fare in hand, and also entered the vehicle, selecting a seat very near the front from which she could watch her quarry and be able to leave on short notice.

"Don't be silly," Rachel reassured herself, "she'll never recognize you. Thirty years, forty pounds, and a full head of hair are great disguises." Nevertheless, she forced herself not to stare at the guard, who had taken a seat further back, on the opposite side next to a window.

The bus crossed Woodhaven Boulevard and continued into areas that seemed older and less affluent than Forest Hills, with small front yards and closely spaced gray or brown wooden houses.

Rather suddenly, gears grinding, the bus swung onto a broader thoroughfare. According to the street signs, they were traveling on Grand Avenue, and the stores' names indicated that they had now arrived in the Maspeth section of Queens.

Finally, at Seventy-First Street, the guard rose and passed right by on her way out. Rachel, still cautious, waited for almost the last minute, and just when the door was about to close, made a hasty exit, nearly tripping on the steps. Some of the driver's words floated down to her.

"Damn idiots . . . Should pay attention and watch . . ."

Rachel was too focused on seeing which direction Steinbrecher took to really notice or care about the invective aimed at her. As she hurried along after the Nazi, she could smell the spicy, pungent aromas that wafted from the open door of a German delicatessen and floated in the air for several yards.

The guard was walking at a brisk pace, swinging the Alexander's bag in an infuriatingly carefree manner. She passed several pedestrians, mostly housewives and young mothers with toddlers or baby carriages. She continued along Grand Avenue, where light traffic glided smoothly by, and turned right at the corner of Seventy-Third Street. Rachel followed, a few steps back, on the other side of the thoroughfare, but it appeared that such prudent behavior was unwarranted. Steinbrecher had never turned her head, not once, to check to see if anyone was behind her.

"Probably," Rachel reasoned, "after all this time she must figure that she's safe, and that no one will ever know that she tortured and murdered innocent people during the war. Maybe something can be done to make her feel a little less secure and chutzpahdik (audacious)!" Rachel muttered under her breath, gnashing her teeth and gripping the strap of her shoulder bag so tightly that her knuckles turned white, as she continued to shadow her quarry.

After two blocks, the guard made a left. She halted briefly to greet an elderly woman who was pushing a shopping cart and wearing a white cardigan over a flowered housedress and "sensible" black shoes with socks.

"Beautiful day, Mrs. Neulander! How are you doing?" Steinbrecher bellowed.

Rachel craned her neck to hear by which name the neighbor would address the guard, but the woman's voice was low and unintelligible.

Steinbrecher, continuing on her way, took out keys from her black leather pocketbook. She approached a small gray house with a neatly manicured lawn that featured a sharply edged border, but lacked the cheery yellow chrysanthemums that blossomed in the front of many neighboring homes.

The high-pitched yapping that greeted their mistress's return had to belong to at least two small dogs, Rachel surmised. Steinbrecher had always kept dogs, but in the camp they had been large and vicious, bloodily ripping the throats out of prisoners unlucky enough to engender the guard's wrath.

"Guten tag, liebe kleine hunde (Good day, dear little dogs)!" Steinbrecher called out laughingly to her pets. The barking reached a crescendo and then suddenly stopped as the door closed with a tinny rattle of the shiny "golden" knocker.

Rachel, still circumspect, stood diagonally across the street behind a parked car and quickly memorized the address that was boldly written in black letters on the brightly painted white mailbox.

Before her departure, she took one last precaution, drawing a blank paper out of her handbag and pretending to study it. Then Rachel raised her eyes to stare at house numbers on both sides of the block. She turned her palms up in feigned bewilderment and stamped her foot in mock anger. Utilizing an expression that she had often heard from her children, she shook her head in frustration and exclaimed very loudly

"Oh, puhleez! Give me a break!" Then she turned sharply on her heel and, still shaking her head, walked with quick, hard steps back in the direction from which she had come.

To any watchful neighbor who might otherwise alert the guard that she was under surveillance, Rachel's charade would cause her to appear to be just another confused, exasperated traveler, lost in the labyrinth of streets, avenues, roads, and drives that comprised the borough of Queens.

As she began to retrace her steps to Grand Avenue, Rachel reflected on the irony that now she and the repulsive guard had something in common—they were both dog owners.

For a long while, Rachel and Isaac had disliked and feared all dogs. Then, about ten years ago, on a cold, dark January afternoon at the start of a blizzard, the children had come into the apartment with a thin, whimpering Airedale mix. Already, snow was beginning to overlay the dog's beige fur, but there was not enough of it to hide a large red gash on the animal's side.

"Please, Mom, can we keep him? He'll die if he stays outside!"

Rachel had shuddered as her thoughts were propelled back in time. The ferocious SS dogs, hateful as their handlers, had seemed to wait, as they pulled at their leashes, with joyous anticipation for the opportunity to inflict torturous deaths on camp inmates.

"No, certainly not," Rachel was about to reply when, with a mother's tender heart, she had regarded the four pairs of pleading eyes—human and canine—that had been focused upon her.

On closer inspection, this stray appeared far from vicious. In fact, he was starving and trembling with fear—two conditions that Rachel strongly identified with.

She had felt something warm and wet, and startled, had looked quickly down.

"See, Mom, he likes you!" Steven had exclaimed, his voice loud with excitement.

The dog was kissing the back of Rachel's hand, like a desperate commoner beseeching an omnipotent monarch for clemency.

Why should these innocents have to pay for the evil perpetrated by the Germans? Moreover, Rachel and Isaac had always attempted, as far as possible, to avoid having their Holocaust experiences impact negatively on their children, and to impart caring, kind behavior.

"Oh, all right!" she had sighed, throwing up her hands in defeat. "But," she had cautioned, using the time-honored mother's mantra, "you'll have to take care of him!"

Even as she had issued the imperative, she had understood its futility. While her pet-loving children's whoops of delight had echoed throughout the apartment, Rachel had started for the medicine cabinet, where the antibiotic ointment was kept. That nasty wound on the stray needed to be looked after. Then she planned to feed him the leftover meatloaf that was in the refrigerator.

Oddly enough, Rachel felt more secure with the protection of a loyal watchdog. But it had been a long time before either she or Isaac could hear Skippy bark without giving an involuntary start.

Exhausted, Rachel sank into the bus's dark green seat for the return trip from the guard's Maspeth neighborhood to Forest Hills. Her brow wrinkled with concentration as she mulled over what she had learned, and considered the most effective use of that information.

Going to the police might not be appropriate. After all, this was an international, not a local, matter. Max, her daughter Mindy's husband, was a lawyer, the son of Hungarian Holocaust survivors, and an up-and-coming leader in the Jewish Defense Coalition, an organization dedicated to combating anti-Semitism in business, education, and the media. They also pressured authorities to bring perpetrators of bias crimes to justice.

"I'll call Max. He'll know what to do," Rachel decided.

But first she would discuss the situation with Isaac.

That night, at dinner, Rachel's beloved specialty, kasha *varnishkes* (kasha with bowties), lacked its usual scrumptious moistness. It tasted too salty, as if a distracted cook hadn't paid close enough attention to the amount of seasonings that she had incorporated into the dish.

"What's wrong, Mom?" Steven asked, noting his mother's silence and her jerky movements as she quickly mopped up the water that had splashed out of a glass she had carried to the table.

"Yeah," agreed Esti, putting down her knife and fork to peer at Rachel. "You haven't said anything at all tonight, and you're not eating."

"Some men might think a woman who doesn't talk is a *mechayeh* (pleasure)!" joked Isaac. Then he looked more closely at Rachel's pale, drawn face. Her whole being appeared tense and coiled, like the Slinky

25

spring toy that his children had played with years before, when they had been small. His laughing demeanor instantly vanished.

"What happened?" he inquired, frowning, his eyes on his wife.

"*Nisht yetz; shpater* (Not now; later)," Rachel answered, her face suddenly flushed.

The dining room table was quickly cleared, and Isaac followed Rachel into the immaculate beige and white kitchen as she arranged the plates and utensils in the dishwasher. When she was finished loading it, she slammed the machine's door shut with such force that the contents rattled loudly.

Skippy had joined the couple in the kitchen, hoping, even after his bounteous dinner, to be treated to any available leftovers. At the sudden, deafening clatter, he raced out, tail between his legs, and found refuge under the coffee table in the living room.

"*Zeby jej krew zala* (May she be covered in [her own] blood)!" Rachel snarled, employing a Polish curse that her husband had never, in all the years that he had known her, heard her use.

"*Vos hut passiert* (What happened)?" he repeated, putting his arms around his wife.

Rachel trembled violently as she recounted her day's discovery.

"You really think it was her?" Isaac questioned, but already his fists were clenched. He was too familiar with his wife's thorough, careful nature to have many doubts.

"*Zicher, dos is zie gevaizen* (Sure, it's her)! The looks, the voice, that scar on her left hand. It *was* her, walking around free as a bird, free as a bird!" Rachel's voice cracked, and she was sobbing as visions of the red-headed sisters came before her eyes.

"Do you realize," she hoarsely reflected as another scathing, long-unused Polish curse flew off her tongue, "that those girls were younger when she killed them than our kids are now? Only because of that *suka* (bitch), they never had a chance to grow up, to have a life?"

Rachel swallowed hard and continued with difficulty, "I thought to call Max. He probably will know the best way to handle this." She looked at her husband for confirmation as she dried her eyes and blew her nose.

"Good idea," agreed Isaac, nodding in assent. "I also think he'll be able to help."

They waited until after 8 o'clock because Max's legal practice often kept him in the office late. Then, with deliberate, forceful motions, Isaac dialed the young couple's number.

"Hi, Mindy. How's my little teacher tonight? You're finished eating?" Isaac greeted his daughter without the usual lilt in his voice.

"Sure we're done, Papa. Anything new?"

"Mom would like to speak to Max, please. She has something to ask him," Isaac replied.

Mindy raised her eyebrows. Isaac and Rachel very rarely sought Max's advice. They had always dreaded being regarded as *"nudgie* (pesty)" in-laws.

"You're sure everything's okay?" Mindy's voice suddenly became more shrill.

"We're all right. Please put Max on," her father repeated his earlier request.

"Sure, Papa. Hold on." Mindy shrugged her shoulders in bewilderment as she handed the phone to Max.

Isaac silently passed the receiver to Rachel. He took her free hand in his and gently squeezed it.

Rachel gave an account of her day's discovery as Max listened attentively and wrote down key points. She tried to keep her voice steady, and not to choke over her words. However, when she completed the story of the murdered sisters, she burst out, "That damn Nazi shouldn't be here; she should be rotting in jail, or better yet, dead!" She banged her hand down hard on the kitchen table.

"You're absolutely sure that it was really her?" Max queried.

Once again Rachel repeated her trifecta of proof in an unsteady voice—the appearance, the voice, the damning scar.

"Oh, and I just realized—she must have a different last name. When I looked at her left hand, I saw a wedding ring," Rachel suddenly recalled.

"We'll take this step by step," Max announced. As he spoke, a plan of action was already forming in his mind, but neither he nor Rachel could project just how serendipitous his involvement would be.

As the Ginsbergs were thanking their son-in-law and wishing him a good night, Steven, searching for some food to fortify him as he studied for an organic chemistry exam, strolled into the kitchen.

"What's new with Mindy and Max?" he inquired, not really looking at his parents, because his immediate focus was on gathering his snacks of choice—a bag of pretzels and a large yellow banana. After her years of starvation, his mother always stocked a plentiful supply of food for her family.

Rachel and Isaac exchanged glances.

"Wait here. I'll get Esti. Mom has something to tell you both," Isaac ordered his son in an unusually loud and commanding voice.

Steven was about to protest that he needed study time for a difficult exam that was to take place the very next day. However, after considering Isaac's urgent tone and the tenor of the evening's meal, he silently took a seat at the kitchen table. He lifted his dark blond head in expectation.

Esti entered right behind Isaac, her black curls bouncing with each step that she took. A *Journal of Physical Therapy* that she had been consulting was still clutched in her hand.

"What's going on?" Esti looked from parent to parent as she sat down.

Isaac took a deep breath and began, "Mom saw someone from *Kriegzeit* (wartime) in Alexander's today."

"Great!" Esti smiled. "Did you remember her from the camp, or is she from Warsaw, too?"

The Ginsberg children were always happy to meet new-found acquaintances from their parents' European background. In their fragment of society, dear friends often filled the roles that normally would have been taken by the relatives who had been murdered.

"No, Esti," Rachel explained, leaning forward in her chair, her voice low and intense. "She wasn't a prisoner. She was a guard who murdered two girls that I knew from my city."

For a moment, her eyes had tears in them. Then she shook her head to help her focus on the present.

"Mommy, how horrible!" Esti stood and quickly moved behind Rachel's chair so that she could drape her arms protectively around her mother.

"Listen," Steven warned, his chemistry exam all but forgotten, "don't go back to Alexander's alone! After midterms, I'll have time, I'll go with you." He put his snack foods down and took his mother's hand.

"Mom has already done something on her own," Isaac looked at his wife. "Tell them," he urged.

Rachel hesitated momentarily. "I followed Steinbrecher, the guard, to her house."

"You did *what?*" both Steven and Esti asked in a loud chorus, their eyes wide.

"Don't worry, she didn't see me. I wanted to know exactly where she lived, so that if something can be done about the situation, she can be easily found. That's what I was speaking to Max about."

Rachel's children stared at her. They had always believed that their mother was strong and clever, but the discovery of such a tremendous amount of courage and resourcefulness left them speechless.

The telephone rang. Even before Isaac answered, everyone knew that it was Mindy. Max would have had just enough time to tell his wife about her mother's encounter with an evil remnant of a tragic past.

"Oh, Mommy," Mindy began in an unsteady voice, "Are you okay?"

A week and a half later, shortly before Rachel was to light the Sabbath candles, Max called from home.

"My detective found out that Steinbrecher is married to a former American soldier, Floyd Harrigan. He was a member of the U.S. forces that occupied Germany. That's where he met her. She came here as a war bride in 1949."

Rachel was aghast. Her eyes widened with disbelief. "That means they let her come to the United States before they let us in!"

"Yeah, they were in a rush to have such an exemplary person become a citizen," Max cracked sarcastically. "But to be fair, she lied on her application, and said that during the war she had been a factory worker. She just neglected to mention that it was a *death* factory." Max spat out the words.

"Anyway," he continued, "This is a good start. We'll keep on digging."

"Thanks, Max," Rachel said, "You did a wonderful job!"

"I feel like I'm doing a *mitzvah* (good deed)," he answered in a quieter voice. "Good *Shabbos!*"

With hope beginning to bud like a newly blossoming flower, Rachel shared the news with her concerned and anxious family. They hugged her and repeated how brave they thought that she was. Then she hurried to light the candles and usher in the Sabbath.

About three weeks after that phone call, on an unseasonably warm late autumn day, Max once again rang up his mother-in-law.

Rachel immediately understood that something extraordinary had developed. Max had always called at night, after work, but now the black kitchen clock showed that it was only eleven-thirty in the morning. His voice was so loud, and he spoke so quickly, that Rachel was tempted to hold the phone away from her ear, which was beginning to hurt from her son-in-law's high decibel tones. As the conversation progressed, she was very glad that she had made the decision to keep the receiver close, and not to risk missing even one word.

"Great news!" Max had exploded. "Our organization has members not only in the United States, but in Europe as well. One of the members over there—he's a wealthy businessman—offered a very substantial reward for documentation that Steinbrecher had been a guard in any of the camps. A bureaucrat in Munich—now a much richer bureaucrat—found some dusty old files hidden in a back room of the state archives."

"Guess what he turned up?" Max nearly shouted. "An ID paper with a picture of Steinbrecher *in Nazi uniform*!!! The document also listed the camps in which she worked." Max paused to catch his breath. "This wealthy European guy is sending copies both to the U.S. Immigration and Naturalization Service, and to me. I should get the papers in a day or two," Max concluded as he pumped his fist high in a gesture of triumph that Rachel could not see.

"Does that mean that they'll throw her out of this country?" Rachel inquired, her voice shaking. She was too numb to feel celebratory. She sank down heavily on a kitchen chair, trying to catch her breath.

"Not yet. There'll be a trial. Her lawyer will probably try to establish that Steinbrecher was just following orders and that the only thing she did was to supervise prisoners in a benign manner—a minor functionary. He will also try to demonstrate that currently she's a model citizen worthy of remaining in the United States. It'll be your job, and the job of any other witnesses that we can find, to testify otherwise. But we have a much stronger case now. Before, it would have been your word against hers. Now, thanks to the German obsession with record—keeping, we have documentation that proves that your identification was definitely *not* a mistake. Everything looks good!"

Max paused for a moment. The secretary had opened the door to his office to check on her boss. She had never heard him speak in such a loud and animated manner. He smiled and waved her away as he concluded the conversation with his mother-in-law.

"Take care. Best to Papa and the kids. I'll speak to you soon!"

"Thanks, Max," Rachel spoke in a low voice. She was too spent to say more. She shook all over as her kitchen whirled around her like an out-of-control carousel.

An hour later, when Steven returned from his after-school job in a veterinarian's office, Rachel was still in the kitchen, sitting motionless.

"It's not fair! She's a nice lady! She lets my kids play with her dogs," exclaimed the stringy-haired, dirty-blond woman, shaking her head in anger. She wrapped her arms protectively around her two elementary-school-age daughters, who snuggled into the folds of their mother's black-and-white buffalo-checked wool jacket.

"Mrs. Harrigan's a good neighbor. She keeps up her property, and she's never bothered anybody. Who cares what she did thirty years ago?" a heavy-set, ruddy-faced man contributed, in answer to a reporter's query.

"Yeah, it's always quiet there," an older neighbor interjected. "That's why when we heard her crying and screaming in German, we didn't understand what she was saying, but we knew something was really wrong. Then they said she got a letter from Immigration. We want her to stay right here! They should throw out the muggers, not her!" His jaw clenched, and he glared into the television camera.

"Right," agreed the beefy homeowner, jutting out his chin defiantly. "People should just mind their own damn business," he concluded, shaking his head.

The defensive rhetoric from her Maspeth neighbors had come after the INS had notified Steinbrecher that her citizenship was in jeopardy, and the media had descended on the blue-collar area for the "human interest" aspect of the story.

The attitude of these Americans, even after they had been informed of the guard's alleged murderous deeds, was disquieting and chilling to Rachel, to Isaac, and to the Jewish community.

"They'd think a lot different if it were their kids . . ." Rachel's dark eyes flashed with anger.

"Or maybe just if it wasn't *Jews* she murdered!" Isaac snarled.

"How come they didn't arrest her and put her in jail right away?" Rachel had inquired in shock when Max received advance news that action would be taken by the government.

Max answered, sighing, "The INS said, quote, 'Mrs. Steinbrecher-Harrigan is not an immediate danger to the public.'" He smiled sardonically.

"Yeah, I'll bet she's a *very* law-abiding citizen, doesn't even cross the street if the light isn't green," Isaac sneered. "She wouldn't want to call unnecessary attention to herself."

"Well, they did take away her passport, though. At least she can't leave the country as a free woman, and if she's found guilty, she may face charges in Germany," Max offered.

"Don't be too sure. Her 'friends' have ways of doing underhanded things. Look at the lawyer she has defending her," Rachel pointed out, shaking her head.

Steinbrecher was to be represented by Randall Kingston, an attorney with a high profile and a higher fee. When his name had been announced, rumors began to circulate in the survivor community that his bill was being paid by an organization of former Nazi Party officers and members. Absolutely nothing that the detective had uncovered when he investigated the Steinbrecher-Harrigans' finances suggested that they could have independently afforded such an expensive advocate.

The pricey lawyer had already been of service. When a television crew waylaid the guard outside her home, Kingston, who was accompanying her, had quickly waved them away and attempted to usher her past the clamorous Fourth Estate. However, a microphone that had been thrust in Steinbrecher's direction picked up her guttural "Verdammte Juden (damn Jews)!" even as her representative quickly pulled the device close to himself and proclaimed in his trademark baritone, "My client will be exonerated!"

Local tabloids had a field day with the story, proclaiming in large headlines, "THE NAZI NEXT DOOR," and "Ma—SS—peth."

After the television story aired, Isaac questioned Max. "Lawyers don't usually go to their clients' homes, do they?"

"No, they don't, but for what this guy's being paid," answered his ever-pragmatic son-in-law, "he should follow her to the gates of hell!"

Max could only nod in agreement with Rachel's point about the guard's Nazi supporters. "Let's hope her German obedience to authority pre-empts her wish to escape and hide out in some remote corner of the U.S."

The family was sitting in the Ginsbergs' mauve and green living room on a frosty Sunday afternoon in December. It was shortly after the INS had announced that there would be a hearing on Steinbrecher's case in the late spring. The information about the guard's past, resulting in pressure from politicians and the media, as well as from Jewish organizations, had forced the agency to act in a decisive, if not terribly timely, manner. At least, Rachel consoled herself, the Service had taken the allegations seriously enough to schedule a court date at which the accusations could be heard and evaluated.

In March, Rachel met with the young and energetic lawyer for the INS, Vincent Scalia. The dark-complexioned, sharply dressed attorney instructed her, "Just tell your story to the judge the same way that you told it to me. Don't be intimidated by Kingston. Garbage like Steinbrecher doesn't deserve to stay in the U.S.," Scalia declared in a raised voice, his brown eyes flashing with indignation.

In an effort to locate witnesses, Max's organization had placed notices in Yiddish, Polish, German, Russian, Hungarian and Hebrew newspapers. They had also sent notices to survivors' groups and *Landsman* (hometown) associations. As a result of that publicity, two other people had come forward to testify to the guard's cruelty.

"Why was there such a poor response to the request for witnesses?" Scalia queried Rachel. "I would think that victims of this monster would be chafing at the bit to testify."

"Almost none of the prisoners who saw Steinbrecher beating and killing survived," Rachel explained. "Of those few who weren't murdered, most would be too emotionally upset to speak about their experiences publicly. Do you know how many of my friends told me not to testify, that it will be too hard on me? And believe me, it will be hard, very hard!" She did not add that she hadn't had a good night's sleep in months, since October, when she had first spotted the guard.

Rachel looked past Scalia out of the building's casement window, but the people and places she saw were not in the present dimension.

"I have to try to get justice, especially for the Feldman sisters. I couldn't live with myself if I didn't!" She stuck out her chin defiantly.

"Good for you. You're doing the right thing!" Scalia nodded his approval. "Your testimony may be the key to a conviction."

"But you have two other witnesses besides me, don't you?"

"Yes, but I'm concerned about them," Scalia confided to Rachel as he pushed his glasses higher on his nose.

"The first witness will be Mr. Nathan Berger, originally from Lodz. He's a frail, older gentleman, and he's still recovering from a heart attack that he suffered six months ago. I can understand why his family is so opposed to his coming to court, but he insists on testifying. When he was here, he was sitting opposite me, where you are now," Scalia motioned across the three-and a-half-foot-wide cherry wood conference table, "and I could hardly hear him. Even with a microphone, I'm not sure how audible he'll be. If everyone, especially the judge and the court reporter, has to strain their ears, and there are constant interruptions for clarification, the power of his testimony will be diluted."

"And that bastard Kingston will keep pushing Mr. Berger. He'll pretend to be all concerned and courteous, but his specialty is rubbing people the wrong way, to shake their stories, and to make them sound unsure and unreliable. Very often the witnesses questioned by him get so rattled that they're unable to complete their testimony."

Scalia brought his hand down hard on the table in frustration.

"Then," he continued, "there's Mrs. Irene Rosenthal. Oh, everyone will hear *her*. Look, I can understand how emotional she'll be; I'm a parent too, but when I interviewed her, she became really hysterical when she described how Steinbrecher sent her son to the gas chamber. Just seeing that Nazi again could send her over the edge! Mrs. Rosenthal might become too overwrought to be cross-examined, and the judge could possibly get the impression that if only Kingston could question her, the 'great' defense lawyer could highlight some inaccuracies in her story."

"So why should these poor people subject themselves to such mental torture if they're not going to help much anyway?" Rachel asked as she shook her head with sympathy for her two potential fellow witnesses.

"Well, I'm giving you the worst case scenarios, but maybe things won't turn out quite as badly as I've projected. I'm hoping for the best, but even if the testimonies are flawed, they can still add a few lines to the portrait of Steinbrecher as a merciless killer. We have to hit them with everything we have, and get her out of the U.S. fast!" To emphasize his point, Scalia banged down several beige manila folders that he had started to pick up.

"I'll see you in May," Scalia paused to consult a black-covered pocket calendar, "the twenty-second, but if you have any questions before then, feel free to give me a call."

As the lawyer escorted Rachel to the elevator bank, the acrid odor of the newly washed floor wafted up and pinched their nostrils. "By the way," he asked as they walked, "are you in the Queens telephone directory?"

"No, we took our names out years ago. Too many people called to sell us too many things we didn't need at dinner time—it was worth every penny not to be bothered! But your secretary has my number, doesn't she? I gave it to her." Had the young girl with the teased black hair and too much make-up lost the information, Rachel wondered with annoyance.

"Oh, sure, we have it," Scalia reassured her, "I was just hoping that you were unlisted so that Steinbrecher's," and here he raised two fingers of each hand to signify quotation marks, "'enthusiasts' don't call and annoy you." Scalia didn't disclose that in cases of all types, witnesses were sometimes intimidated into not testifying by threats of violence to themselves or to their families. It would be better for everyone, he thought with relief, if Rachel was difficult to locate. He shook hands with her as an elevator car arrived.

"Thank you for all of your hard work. Stay well," she called out as she entered.

"You, too!"

Rachel turned in time to see Scalia raise his hand in farewell.

She waved back as the elevator door silently slid shut, but she was worried. She knew that many more sleepless nights awaited, and that she would need to be at the top of her game to stand up to the formidable Randall Kingston.

Rachel was suddenly reminded of a television interview with the very organized and capable wife of the state's governor. When asked for the secret of her efficiency, the former schoolteacher had raised her voice for emphasis and replied, "Try not to do things when you're tired, because that's when you'll make mistakes!"

As her heels clicked against the marble floor of the lobby and she exited the building, Rachel prayed that when she returned for the hearing, she would not be too exhausted to do a credible job and finally obtain a modicum of justice for Steinbrecher's victims.

The INS occupied a modern glass building on a wind-swept corner in lower Manhattan. For the hearing, the agency had designated a small, white-walled room with five double rows of shiny wooden seats that were softened by bright green cushions. It was assumed that only a day or two would be needed for the testimony.

The long-awaited morning dawned chilly and gray, as if nature itself was mourning those whom the guard had mercilessly killed. Rachel was glad that she had decided to wear a warm black wool suit and pink sweater underneath, even though such an outfit was not an obvious choice for the middle of May.

The Ginsbergs had arrived early. Only Max was absent from Rachel's strong support group, because of a crucial court case in his own legal practice that could not be rescheduled. There had been no instructions as to which seats to select, so Rachel and her family decided to occupy places in the middle of the room. From there, they had an excellent view of those who had come to observe and participate in the hearing.

There were reporters and two staff artists (no cameras were permitted) from newspapers and television. A group of about ten teenagers, wearing leather jackets, *yarmulkas* (skullcaps), and arm bands from the militant JAAS (Jews Against Anti-Semitism) group swaggered in. They were hoping to intimidate the Nazi, and to show the Jewish community's solidarity with the victims. The Ginsbergs nodded with approval and appreciation.

While the room was not completely filled, most seats had been quickly occupied, and so Rachel was deprived of the opportunity to wait together with the other witnesses.

Steinbrecher entered with her husband and her lawyer, Randall Kingston. Rachel, Isaac, Mindy, Esti, and Steven joined the militant group in glaring at the Nazi woman. Their eyes narrowed with hatred as they watched the couple being guided to a front seat by the famous attorney.

The guard was dressed neatly in a beige polyester suit and white blouse. Her husband, Floyd Harrigan, was a slender, mature-looking

American with thinning salt-and-pepper hair. He appeared to be three or four inches shorter than his wife. Incredibly, under his brown sports jacket, he was wearing the very gray shirt that Rachel had observed Steinbrecher buying that fateful day in Alexander's. The couple's obviously inexpensive clothing served to remind Rachel who was probably paying Kingston's exorbitant bill.

As she looked at the Nazi, Rachel, whose stomach was already queasy with tension, felt a sharp wave of nausea. Isaac instantly sensed his wife's upset and put his arm around her. She could only nod weakly at Scalia when he came over to greet her and her family.

At exactly ten o'clock Geoffrey Northrup, the hearing officer, called the proceedings to order.

The first witness, Mr. Nathan Berger, a widower, had worked for twenty-five years as a tailor in Brooklyn. The stooped gait of the diminutive survivor reflected his hard years as a slave laborer, and emphasized the illnesses that had resulted from such long-term abuse of his body. Mr. Berger's tall blond daughter escorted him as he shuffled up to the witness stand. She returned to her seat reluctantly, and only after she was reassured by her father several times that he was feeling well and was ready to tell his story to the court.

In a low, thin voice, Nathan Berger testified that Steinbrecher had beaten him as he exited the cattle car that had transported him and hundreds of others to the camp. His first wife and two children had already been shot in the ghetto of Lodz, he explained to Scalia, as tears coursed down his cheeks.

Then it was Kingston's turn to question the witness. After his preliminary "greeting," the attorney got down to work.

"You claim that Mrs. Harrigan beat you. Isn't it true that she just pushed you with her hand so that you would move along? She didn't 'attack' you with anything else at all, did she?"

"She beat me with a *dubinka*," the tailor replied, his voice growing weaker with each word. "I'm sorry, sir, I don't know how to say in English."

Kingston turned his palms up in a gesture of futility. A mocking smile played about his lips, as if to say, "How can we take this witness seriously, if he can't make himself understood?"

"Truncheon!" Isaac stood and called out in a loud, clear voice. "She beat him with a truncheon!"

Momentarily, all eyes in the room were turned in Rachel's husband's direction.

"Thank you," Kingston acknowledged the translation, the smile quickly fading from his face. He had obviously hoped that there would be no description of the guard's weapon, or at least a far less damaging one.

However, he was undeterred, and he quickly assumed another tack.

"There were many guards supervising when the trains were unloaded, were there not?"

"Yes sir." The witness's reply was barely audible.

"And you were exhausted, hungry, and thirsty after the long train ride. Is that correct?"

"Yes, sir."

"And yet," a note of sarcasm crept into Kingston's voice, "you're so sure that it was Mrs. Harrigan who beat you?"

"I could NEVER FORGET that mean face!"

The words were the loudest that the witness had spoken, but the effort took its toll on him. Nathan Berger took a small brown bottle from his jacket. He quickly opened it, removed a nitroglycerine tablet, and inserted it under his tongue. His testimony, and the memories that it conjured, was causing the angina that his doctor had cautioned him about.

Kingston pressed on, "You never saw Mrs. Harrigan actually kill anyone, did you?"

The witness didn't answer. Even after ingesting the pill, he was pale. He appeared to have trouble catching his breath.

"Please answer the question, Mr. Berger," Kingston insisted.

"Objection!" Scalia shouted. "Counsel is—"

Nathan Berger's daughter sprang out of her seat and nearly ran to her father's side.

"That's it! Please excuse him! You're not going to kill my papa!" She quickly took her father's arm and escorted him out of the room, pausing only to give Steinbrecher a withering look.

Rachel's and Isaac's mouths tightened with anger at Kingston's relentless badgering of the pitiful witness, and because Nathan Berger was unable to complete his answer to Kingston's leading question.

Scalia, however, was not totally displeased.

"Look, at least he established the fact that Steinbrecher beat him with a heavy weapon. The unfortunate part is that we weren't able to explain that Berger had never seen her kill anyone only because he was in the men's part of the camp, and had had no further contact with her. It could have been worse." Scalia smiled to encourage Rachel. He was glad he had decided to save her testimony, which he had judged to be the strongest, for last. It would be good for the case to conclude on a powerful note.

Mrs. Irene Rosenthal was the next witness. She presented herself well, with frosted-blond hair and a stylish navy pantsuit. Her second husband, two post-war children, and a sister who had, Rachel later learned, survived the Holocaust in Siberia accompanied her.

Scalia deftly elicited details of her four-year-old son's seizure by Steinbrecher, as Mrs. Rosenthal spoke softly but, at first, coherently through her tears.

"We had just arrived at the camp. When she saw my little boy hiding behind my skirts, he was so scared, she took him and flung him on a truck with children that were on their way to the gas chamber. I tried to fight her, but she was much stronger than I was. We hadn't had much food in the ghetto, and what I got I shared with my son. I just didn't have the strength to save him." She bowed her head.

"Do you see the guard who took your son from you in this room?" Scalia asked softly.

"*She's sitting RIGHT OVER THERE!*" Mrs. Rosenthal shrieked in a loud voice and pointed, her finger shaking, to Steinbrecher, who sat with an impassive expression on her face.

The witness sobbed as Scalia thanked her for her testimony.

It was Kingston's time to cross-examine.

In his deceptively gentle southern drawl, Kingston asked Mrs. Rosenthal, "Now, you testified that Mrs. Harrigan sent your son to the gas chamber. How do you know that? Perhaps she was just seeing that he was taken to a hospital?"

"He wasn't sick! He only wanted to stay with me, and she sent him away to be killed! I never saw him again! Oh, my poor Avrum Yaakov! My sweet baby!" Irene Rosenthal screamed as she rocked with grief.

The now-hysterical mother was crying uncontrollably. Her last words were so distorted by her sobs and shrieks that they were almost unintelligible. She would not, could not continue, so Kingston's heartless insinuation that perhaps her boy had been taken away to be hospitalized went virtually unchallenged.

"*Momzer* (bastard)," Isaac muttered, in a curse that was intended to describe both the guard and her lawyer. Rachel's eyes glittered with tears. Mindy, Esti, and Steven could only shake their heads in sympathy with the bereaved woman. Now, more than ever, after witnessing the merciless defense attorney in action, they were very concerned as they anticipated the difficulties that awaited their mother on the witness stand. They could not imagine the shocking turn of events that lay just ahead.

Judge Northrup declared a lunch recess.

When court resumed, Rachel would be the final witness.

There wasn't any kosher food available in the vicinity of the hearing, so Rachel had packed a bountiful lunch for her family.

As they sat in the brightly lit cafeteria of the INS building, Mindy exclaimed, "That Kingston is so disgusting! Did you see how he kept calling her *Mrs. Harrigan* and never used her German name? It looked like he was trying to whitewash her, and to make her into a wholesome all-American!!" Mindy spat out the words.

"You sound like Max," Esti said, paying tribute to the acuity of her sister's observation.

"Thanks. It's like he's dipping a skunk in perfume!" Mindy continued to rail.

Steven tried to lighten the mood. "Watch what you say," he cautioned his sister. "The skunks might get offended!"

The girls and Isaac laughed briefly.

Rachel made no comment. She had barely touched the food she had prepared because she was too preoccupied with the specter of Mrs. Rosenthal, who had been instantaneously transformed from a soignée and poised fashionista to a hysterical mourner by the relentless Kingston.

The hearing resumed at two o'clock.

With a superhuman effort, Rachel walked to the witness stand with her head high. As she took her seat, her hands were clasped tightly together so that no one, especially Kingston, could see that they were shaking. In front of Rachel's eyes, everything in the room seemed to be floating in space, like objects in a Chagall painting.

Guided by Scalia, she told the story of the Feldman sisters in a calm, subdued voice.

Then it was time for the defense to cross-examine.

"Good afternoon, Mrs. Ginsberg," Kingston began, smiling. He angled his rangy six-foot frame toward Rachel and lowered his head closer to her level in the witness chair. Rachel felt as if the lawyer was intruding into her personal space. Was this his strategy to intimidate her? She sat up even straighter.

"Isn't it true that you suffered from typhus in the camp?" questioned Kingston.

Even though he had no knowledge of Rachel's personal health history, it was a fairly safe assumption that she had been a victim of the disease. Most of the starved, weakened survivors contracted this illness, which had been epidemic in the crowded, filthy conditions in the prisoners' barracks.

"Yes," Rachel replied in a clear, strong voice.

"And isn't it also true that one of the manifestations of typhus is the experiencing of hallucinations?"

"Often, yes," Rachel replied warily. She could feel the guard's piercing blue eyes boring into her.

"So then," said Kingston, slowly building toward his point, "isn't it possible that you hallucinated this whole episode, and that Mrs. Harrigan did nothing to harm these sisters?"

The attorney raised one arm over his head and looked towards the ceiling, as if he was observing an ephemeral illusion. Then he glanced over at Northrup, as if he was sharing a secret with him. Kingston was actually smirking.

What?!?! Rachel couldn't believe her eyes and ears. The defense lawyer was actually suggesting that the murder of the Feldman girls had never really occurred! It was almost as though he was killing them for a second time. *How dare he?!?* Obviously, Kingston expected Rachel to follow the path of the other witnesses, and to dissolve into a weeping mass of jelly as a result of his infuriating, fabricated, and disrespectful implications.

The attorney had gone too far this time!

White hot anger rose up before Rachel's eyes. It blocked out the guard, the spectators and lawyers, the judge, and even Isaac and her children. She saw only the faces of the Feldman sisters, and members of her own family who had murdered by merciless Nazis, Nazis like

41

Steinbrecher. Rachel's heart was beating loudly, and she was breathing hard. The room, which had seemed uncomfortably cool only a short time before, had suddenly grown very warm.

Someone was answering the attorney in hard, metallic tones. It was a second or two before Rachel realized that it was her own voice that was replying.

"Do you also think that I'm imagining the scar on her hand that I described, a scar that's so light that unless I already knew it was there before, I never would have been able to see?"

"Please, Mrs. Ginsberg, I'll ask the questions." A visibly annoyed Kingston forced a tiny laugh, even as his forehead broke out in a cold sweat.

"I'm just trying to answer your ridiculous story!" Rachel snapped. She looked over to the judge. "May I continue?"

"Yes, go ahead, Mrs. Ginsberg," Northrup nodded his assent.

"I'm sure," Rachel narrowed her eyes and slightly tilted her head to one side, "that you tried very hard to locate the Feldman girls to discredit my testimony."

She could see by the way Kingston gave a start and opened his mouth and eyes in surprise at the acuity of her observation that she had scored a direct hit.

"So where are they?" Rachel demanded. "If they're still alive, and I only imagined their murder, why couldn't you find them?"

"Thank you, Mrs. Gins . . . ." The defense lawyer was trying to rush Rachel off the stand.

"But I haven't finished," she protested in a voice as sharp as a precision knife. "If you had studied anything about typhus (Rachel used the European pronunciation "tee-foos") or spoken to someone who had it, you would understand that the hallucinations are like nightmares— very real while you're sick, but after, you know that they *never actually happened!*" Rachel curled her lip with contempt at the lawyer's ignorance. Her expression of disdain was not lost on anyone in the room.

"*Those poor girls were murdered* EXACTLY THE WAY I TOLD THIS COURT!"

"I was just lucky," she continued, remembering Mindy's point about Kingston using the guard's American name, "that I only caught typhus right *after* liberation, or I couldn't have stood up on the Appelplatz, and Irma Steinbrecher would have killed me, too!"

Rachel's eyes flashed in Kingston's direction as he hastily excused her, and Northrup concluded the hearing by bringing down his gavel with a sharp crack.

Isaac almost ran to her as she came from the witness stand. He embraced her, and was followed by Mindy, Esti, and Steven, who hugged their mother tightly.

"You did a great job, Mom!"

Scalia was next, pumping Rachel's hand up and down with enthusiasm.

"You definitely have to think about going to law school. You really had Kingston upset! It's probably the first time that ever happened to him—in a courtroom, anyway!"

The INS attorney beamed at Rachel. He was delighted to have assessed her ability to be an effective witness correctly. She had practically made his case singlehandedly.

As Rachel was surrounded by the JAAS teenagers, who were offering their congratulations to her, she saw Steinbrecher, her husband Floyd Harrigan, and the slumped Randall Kingston disappear through the door.

There would be months of appeals, Rachel knew, but Scalia told the Ginsbergs he felt confident that ultimately the case would be adjudicated in the INS's favor, and Steinbrecher would be forced to leave the U.S.

In the time after the hearing, Rachel was pleased to note some positive developments. Because of the media coverage, she and some of her friends had been asked to speak about their concentration camp experiences at various schools, centers, and organizations. A local community college had announced plans to establish a library of Holocaust volumes under one roof, so that research on the topic could be more easily conducted. The institution was also starting to offer courses on the subject of the extermination of the Jews. The hope was that when the full power of hatred was understood, more people would at least attempt to tolerate others who were "different" from themselves, so that ethnic annihilation would never again occur.

Best of all, Mindy had given birth to a baby girl. Rachel and Isaac were overjoyed to be grandparents, and to have lived to see the continuity of their families to the third generation.

The entire Ginsberg family floated into Mindy's hospital room on a bubble of joy as soon as visiting hours began. They were laden down with balloons, flowers, and baby gifts. The excitement had begun with a 7 a.m. call from Max announcing the good news. It had been a wonderful surprise; Mindy was not supposed to have given birth for some weeks yet.

"We stopped by the nursery down the hall on our way here and saw the baby. She's beautiful! *Mazel tov* (Congratulations)!" They almost shouted with excitement at the beaming Mindy and Max as they hugged and kissed the new parents. Even though Mindy's roommate was still in "delivery," the small room seemed very crowded by the presence of the Ginsberg family members.

"You're sure you're all right?" Rachel peered closely at her daughter. "You're not in any pain?"

"I'm fine Mommy, really," Mindy laughed. "I'm just relieved that it's over!"

"It's amazing! She's so perfect and not small at all, even though she was a little premature! I have a gorgeous niece!" exclaimed Esti, grinning widely.

"And *I* have a confession," Mindy admitted, lowering her head. She was sitting on the edge of the hospital bed, wearing a pink striped robe. "The baby isn't as early as you think!" A mischievous smile played over her lips.

"Mommy, a few weeks before the hearing, I found out that I was pregnant, but we didn't tell you. You wouldn't have let me come down to the INS; you would have thought that it would be too stressful for me, but I just *had* to be there for you! And then after, I felt so badly that I hadn't been honest about when the baby was due, I couldn't bring myself to tell you the truth, but now that she's here . . . I'm so sorry!"

"You are definitely forgiven! You can't imagine what it meant to me that you, and everyone," Rachel moved her hands in a wide gesture to encompass her whole family, "came with me and gave me the strength to tell exactly what that Nazi murderer had done! But you were right. I would have worried about you *and* the baby if I had known that you were pregnant, and I already had enough to think about! You did the right thing!"

Tension seemed to evaporate from Mindy's body as she relaxed with relief.

"Anyway," the new mother continued, "I was thinking. You said no one from the Feldmans survived, right?"

"Right," Rachel agreed, nodding. Her voice suddenly became lower and sadder. "Those who weren't killed in the ghetto were murdered in the camps."

"So," Mindy explained, "Max and I discussed it, and even though we also have plenty of people in our family that don't have names yet (no one had been named after them), with your permission, we'd like to call the baby 'Sarah Blima'—Sarah Brooke in English—for the Feldman girls so that they and their story are never forgotten."

"Mindy," Rachel embraced her daughter and son-in-law. The words stuck in her throat and were difficult to articulate as she sobbed, "*Sehr schain! Sehr schain!* (How beautiful! How nice!)" She looked at Mindy and Max. "I have wonderful children," she sniffed.

Isaac nodded with approval. "Now those poor girls can rest in peace."

"If Max and I can be half as good to the baby as you and Papa were to us, she'll be a very lucky girl!" Mindy said, smiling at her husband and hugging her parents and siblings again.

"And don't forget, when she's a little older, I'll be happy to teach her all about taking care of cats and dogs!" Steven laughed, as he and Esti attempted to make room for the pink and silver balloon arrangement on the narrow bedside table.

One morning in late October, just a little over a year after she had first seen Steinbrecher in Alexander's, Rachel, restless as usual, awoke before six. She still experienced trouble sleeping in the months after the hearing had concluded, although her nightmares had somewhat subsided. Now she was also overtired from helping Mindy with her two-week-old baby. Even the joyous excitement of being a grandmother interfered with her slumber.

It was unseasonably cool in the apartment, but the slanting rays of the morning sun were already beginning to warm the white ceramic tiles on the kitchen floor. Rachel put up the coffee and switched on an all-news radio station. As the beverage's bittersweet aroma began to fill the room, the irritatingly perky voice of the reporter recited the headlines at the top of the hour. Rachel half-listened as she re-cleaned the already pristine kitchen counters until one news item seemed to reach out and seize her violently by the shoulders.

"Irma Steinbrecher, a former death camp guard, has lost her final appeal to remain in the U.S. She will be deported to her native Germany, where she will stand trial for war crimes. In our other top stories . . ."

Rachel turned off the radio and murmured, *"Baruch Ha Shem* (Blessed is the Name)" as she breathed a sigh of relief and expelled much of the tension that had been bottled up inside her since the whole episode with the Nazi began. She held little hope that Steinbrecher would see much time in prison. Even more vicious killers had somehow been shown the more merciful side of German justice, but at least the guard would not be permitted to live a peaceful existence in the U.S.

The decision, Rachel assumed, had come down very late the preceding night, past the time that Scalia had closed his office. She expected him to call her a bit later, as soon as he learned of the guard's fate, to discuss this latest development in the case. In the meantime, she would let her family, who were also feeling sleep-deprived, get another hour of rest before awakening them to share the good news.

Rachel called Skippy to come for his walk. The old dog was more limber today, probably because of the drastic drop in humidity.

As they exited the lobby and emerged into the building's driveway, Rachel lifted her head and breathed the clear, cool air that had just taken on a fresher, purer quality. She looked up at the slowly rising sun and permitted herself a smile

Fragments

of

American Life

THE VIEW FROM UFT HEADQUARTERS—QUEENS

Recessed lighting fixtures
Reflected on windows
Like sharply angled clouds
Floating in azure mist
Over brown-gray buildings
Black and white rooftops
Lines of light towards the horizon
Stretching to other places
Reaching to other lives.

BRONX VISIONS

Much of the South Bronx has been rebuilt. However, the area that I visited as a child to celebrate Passover still remains a victim of urban blight.

Pueblos with blown-out windows, glass now shattered,
Like vacant eye sockets without life.
Bricks aged to the color of dried blood,
Garbage, spilling out of rusty metal cans,
Crumpled papers, broken sails on concrete seas.
Buildings tattooed by glaring graffiti.
Where is the Bronx of childhood memory?
Here Passover began with an orange-red sun
That bathed narrow, neat streets in copper light
Like the flashing flames of Egypt's furnaces.
My Bronx family, reunited
To recount the ancient tale of freedom,
Insulated in small, overheated rooms
By matzoh, sponge cake, heavy wine, and love.
Where I looked out through the cool black silk of night,
Facing east, towards the Triboro Bridge,
Outlined by its glittering diamond-stud lights,
And imagined that I could really see,
The sparkling, silvery stars of Jerusalem.

THE ROAD NOT TAKEN

Was she actually writing about *him*? Was such an amazing coincidence possible?

I quickly turned to the cover page of the story "The Road Not Taken"—this week's assignment, based on the Frost poem—to re-check Judith's last name. Yes, there it was in bold black print that contrasted sharply with the pristine white page—"Berger."

Just in time, my right hand covered my mouth and smothered the sound—not a gasp really, but a sharp, potentially loud intake of breath that had nearly escaped.

My eyes quickly shifted to my fellow students. None of them had seemed to notice anything strange. All of their heads were bent with deep concentration over copies of the manuscript that Judith was reading to us—a group of retired teachers in this union-sponsored creative writing class.

Most of the works shared here described nostalgic excursions into the past, professional experiences (positive and negative), and the beauty of nature's wonders. There was even a smattering of mysteries, science fiction, as well as exciting war diaries and fascinating Asian and African tales. The presentations reflected the varying levels of skill and creativity of their authors.

The utilitarian fourth-floor Forest Hills, New York, classroom that was our meeting place overlooked congested, multi-lane Queens Boulevard. From time to time the more strident traffic sounds drifted up to disrupt our concentration. This stark venue ostensibly lacked the cushy, soft furniture and quiet atmosphere that might relax body and mind enough to inspire the sharing of confidences. Nevertheless, Judith was chronicling her emotionally traumatic marriage in heart-breaking detail.

Only once before this reading had she given us an indication of the anguish that she experienced. At the very first meeting, when we had introduced ourselves, she had plaintively begged, "Please, never call me Judy!"

The diminutive seemed too carefree, too youthful, too cute to suit her present psychological state, she had explained apologetically, but had hesitated to elaborate further. Finally, today we would learn the rationale behind her polite but emphatic request.

Once again, I furtively scanned my classmates' faces. Many eyebrows were raised in surprise. More than half of our sessions together had already passed, and Judith had been so quiet until today! Perhaps she finally felt comfortable enough, because of the caring, supportive atmosphere, to share her deeply personal revelations.

As she read, I carefully reassessed her. Judith was a short, substantially overweight woman whose petite frame was nearly drowned in an ocean of fat. Her short gray hair framed delicate, remarkably unbloated features. In class, she had once shyly mentioned that in her youth she had enjoyed a promising career as a ballerina. I was not surprised, because I had already noted the grace with which, despite her considerable bulk, she wove her way between the closely placed pieces of green metal classroom furniture. Under the industrial-style track lighting, she had seemingly floated to her seat.

But there was nothing light about Judith's presentation of today. She was recounting the sad saga of her unfortunate union with a mesmerizing but manipulative Frenchman who convinced her to give up her passion—ballet—to be his wife. She had been young, naïve, and so drugged by the narcotic of love that she had reluctantly agreed to his demands.

The marriage produced three sons whom Judith cherished, but it was terribly marred by her husband's duplicity, philandering, and controlling ways.

Judith wrote plaintively of the many nights that she had stayed up late waiting for his return from "working dinners." Those hours, as they dragged on, had been laden with boring television fare and disturbing misgivings. During those waits, Judith recalled in a low voice, she could actually "hear music and see myself gliding across the stage as the spotlights illuminated the lacy edges of my ballet costume."

She had closed her eyes to the tell-tale signs of betrayal. She laughed that she had been in the big Egyptian river—Da Nile—but the laugh cracked, she didn't smile, and her eyes glittered hard for a moment.

After years of the husband's "business trips," over which time she had gained sixty pounds as she eased her loneliness with Haagen Dazs, Judith finally became sick of the state of doubt and self-pity that had sent a pall of depression over her existence and defined her life. She had hired a private detective. This decision, Judith explained, was made easier by the fact that her boys were already independent, and that she had taken courses (against her husband's strongly stated wishes) to enable her to qualify for a New York City teaching license in physical education.

The private eye had come up with irrefutable evidence of her husband's unfaithfulness. The sleuth's overseas contact had even discovered that he had been cheating on his Parisian mistress with a new love in Marseilles!

Neither the husband's Gallic charm nor his sisters' pleading could dissuade Judith from seeing an attorney.

Now she was a divorcee, mourning her youthful love and lost career as she looked bitterly back at "The Road Not Taken."

Once again, just to be sure, I verified the facts in her story, including the names of her ex-husband and his sisters, his age, profession, family history (his family had settled in France after World War I), and his favorite sports.

Then I knew, without a doubt, that Judith had been married to Michael—my first love and former fiancé.

January 1963

"SATURDAY NIGHT SNOW HOP—PRESENTED BY CAMEO HOUSEPLAN," the poster proclaimed. (Houseplans were the more economical, less restrictive versions of sororities. They existed in the New York City municipal college system.)

Hunter College's South Lounge was filled with pink, green, and yellow balloons that contrasted harshly with the room's basic hideous décor—black and white checkered linoleum flooring topped by deep, glaringly bright salmon walls.

The cool air was saturated with the starchy, salty odor of potato chips. Music pulsated scratchily from a phonograph operated by a houseplan volunteer. Indeed, the ancient hi-fi—a donation from the family of one of the members—desperately required a change of needle, which was why I left my post as co-cashier for a short while. Although generally mechanically challenged, I—Maddie, the technical idiot-savant—had developed a unique skill with this phonograph.

Once again, evenly flowing, pleasant sounds began to fill the large, crowded room as I returned to my position near the door. I had been sitting there for only a short while when I felt a light tap on my shoulder.

"Are cashiers allowed to dance?" a deep, smooth, accented voice teasingly asked.

I looked up into dark eyes that sparkled in an olive-skinned face crowned by jet black hair. Even though I was seated, I could estimate the speaker's height at about six feet, and I could judge that he was solidly built. A gorgeous guy!

"Thank you, if Fran will cover for me . . ." I replied as I slowly rose. I hoped that my voice was not trembling with excitement.

"Sure," Fran smiled. It was an unwritten law that girls should assist one another in meeting members of the opposite sex.

"I'm Michael Berger. I didn't see you when I came in," my new friend grinned down as he guided me to the dance floor.

"I was away for a few minutes. I had to change the needle." I motioned towards the phonograph, which was now playing Steve Lawrence's "Go Away, Little Girl," a soft, romantic song.

"Ah, efficient as well as beautiful," Michael murmured.

Suddenly, I was extremely glad that I had set my dark hair with beer (for extra hold), and that I had worn my flattering new black and red wool dress from Alexander's Department Store.

Michael led me gently but firmly, with a slow, easy grace. Even though I was five-foot-five, I felt like a small, delicate doll in his arms. I smiled as I inhaled the sweet fragrance of my perfume, Helena Rubinstein's "Apple Blossom Time" that slowly rose to envelope us.

"Go away, little girl, before I beg you to stay!" I sang along with the hit record. This evening was turning out far better than I had ever expected!

Later, Michael and I sat on a chartreuse couch near a large window that faced Park Avenue. As we looked out, the street, bathed in moonlight that softly illuminated the previous day's snow, was transformed into a fantasyland, and the Russian Embassy, directly across, appeared to be a glittering castle.

"There is a road in Spanish Harlem" blared from the phonograph, but to me, Park Avenue had just turned into a street in paradise.

"Isn't it lovely, chérie?" Michael asked, looking deeply into my eyes. He squeezed my hand briefly, and the warmth of his touch took my breath away.

I subsequently learned that Michael (Michel at home) was twenty-five, and had come from Paris to attend the Columbia Graduate School of Engineering. Recently, he had begun to work for a French firm in Manhattan.

By the time that he had driven me home to Queens, we had arranged to see each other again, for a museum date the very next day.

I was already in love.

The next few months were the happiest that I had ever known.

We spent hours in darkened village coffee houses discussing politics. Even though Michael's training was in the technical field, I discovered that he had a sharp grasp of world events.

We also went to parties, concerts, and shows. With each date, we seemed to grow closer. Classes became just annoying intervals between times spent with Michael.

One day, after school, while Michael was still at work, I visited my high school friend, Naomi. I can still recall sitting on her terrace as I shyly told her about my new love. The gentle spring air teased my nerve endings and heightened my longing for Michael.

The fiery red late afternoon sun was surrounded by a yellow halo that imparted a three—dimensional, spherical quality to it. The intensity of the sky's colors seemed to reflect my own passion.

Early in May, Michael and I became engaged. We planned to fly to Paris late in August, after I had completed summer school, so that I could meet his family. Michael had already charmed *my* family, as well as my friends, with his continental charm and sophistication.

My mother, almost as giddy with excitement as I was, began to plan a December wedding that was to take place right before my January graduation.

A beautiful emerald-cut diamond ring sparkled on my finger. I was very aware as I strode, head held high, through the drab brown college cafeteria, that I was the embodiment of the Hunter girl's dream—handsome, professional fiancé, beautiful ring, degree nearly attained. How could I not be ecstatic?

Perhaps I was a little too self-satisfied to remember that pride goes before a fall.

My mother always said that nothing in this life is perfect, and of course she was right. I learned, as my relationship with Michael deepened, that he possessed many incredible qualities—intelligence, humor, charm, and generosity—but that he also had a roving eye.

I attributed this disconcerting characteristic to his French background. I inwardly vowed not to behave as an immature, insecure American, but to adopt the attitude of a worldly, tolerant European, and so I tried to hide my unhappiness when Michael's gaze targeted an attractive female. He would follow her movements as she walked, his head swiveling like a plant exhibiting a tropism. If he happened to catch her eye, he would grin slowly and seductively. Although I had always been blessed to receive compliments about my own good looks, I began to experience serious self-doubts.

Most of the time, during and after an episode of Michael's less than devoted behavior, I was successful in smiling indulgently, as one would regard a naughty four-year-old. On a few, rare occasions, I was not up to giving Oscar-worthy performances. At those times, Michael would take note of my discomfort, hug me, and laugh, "Maddie, you are feeling neglected!"

But he never stopped looking and he never stopped flirting.

June 1963

The club was suitably darkened for romantic dancing. The ubiquitous cloud-like puffs of cigarette smoke were tinted delicate shades of pink, yellow, and green by the dance floor lights as they slowly rose high in the stuffy room with the flocked red wallpaper.

Michael and I were part of a large group of his friends—we usually went with his friends—some French, some American.

Immediately, I noticed one of the French girls, Simone, whom I had not previously met. She was outstandingly attractive, with dark hair and almond eyes, and a petite, curvy figure. Her charms were certainly not lost on Michael, either, I observed with alarm, as he kept turning to stare in her direction. Glumly, I sipped at my Pink Lady cocktail.

Most of the couples at our table were already dancing, and I was hoping that we could join them on the crowded floor. The three-piece band was playing "Tonight" from *West Side Story,* one of my favorite songs, but Michael excused himself to go to the men's room.

After a few minutes of sitting alone in the semi-darkness, I decided to visit the ladies' lounge to check my make-up. I couldn't permit Simone to outshine me!

The restroom was painted gray, and not much better illuminated than the rest of the club. Probably, I decided with a resigned sigh, I would only smear the cosmetics that defined my green eyes and create a mess in the process, if I attempted to retouch them.

Somewhat annoyed, I quickly went out, but momentarily I lost my sense of direction in the dimly lit corridor. And so it was that I turned left, toward a Jell-O-red exit sign, instead of right, to return to the table.

At first, I saw only the shadows. The two people were so intent on their conversation that they never even noticed me. For a moment, between "Maria" and "There's a Place for Us," the music paused, and I recognized Michael's voice. The other person turned slightly in my direction for an instant, and as her face was caught by a stray, faint beam of light I was able to identify the seductive, sexy Simone.

I slowly edged closer, pushing myself into the shadowed recess of a supply room doorway.

Simone murmured, "Deux-six-un-six-quatre-un-un," and I understood enough French to know that she was giving her phone number to Michael.

Don't jump to conclusions, I cautioned myself, although I could hear my heart begin to pound loudly, *there could be any number of reasons that he would need to contact her. Why, it could be something to do with work, or a mutual friend, or—*

At that moment, my conjectures abruptly ended as the two distinct shadows merged into one amorphous monster. Michael was bending and kissing Simone with deep, twisting motions as her arms slowly wound around his neck.

I was frozen with horror for one terrible moment. Then I quickly turned away, almost doubling over with stabbing pains in my midsection. The corners of my eyes burned, and the taste of the Pink Lady rose in my throat. I walked very carefully because I was trembling violently, and a klutzy fall in the darkness, sure to attract attention, would be a disaster.

I desperately needed to return to the table and alone, attempt to see beyond the powdered fragments of my broken heart, and to concentrate on making a sensible decision. One way or another, I realized, my choices of that night would have a tremendous impact on the rest of my life.

Each additional minute of Michael's absence felt like another punch in the stomach—similar to the pain that I had experienced when a clumsy girl in gym class had thrown a poorly aimed medicine ball that had hit me in my abdomen. However, I was also grateful for the time to consider the ramifications of Michael's actions, and to plan my strategy.

Over the years, when I looked back, I was constantly amazed at my clarity of thought and newly discovered cleverness in response to the soul-shattering events of that evening.

Michael returned quite a while later. He seemed completely cool and unselfconscious, I noted with disgust as he straightened his red—striped tie. (Imported from France, of course!)

"Michael," I began.

"Chérie, I'm really sorry I left you alone for so long, but I met a friend from Paris, you know, and we had much catching up to do."

He moved his head to one side and smiled charmingly. I noted that as he spoke, he slipped a small piece of paper that he had been carrying into his jacket—Simone's number, no doubt.

Yeah, I saw how you were catching up! I thought furiously.

"Oh, I understand, Michael," I smiled softly, shocked at my *own* aptitude for duplicity, "but we have to talk later."

"Tell me now, Maddie; you are making me anxious."

"No, a night club is not the place. Later, in the car," I said a little louder, in a firmer voice than Michael had ever heard me use. I shook my head for emphasis.

Michael nodded, but he shifted in his chair, and his mouth tightened. For the first time, I had an unsettling insight as to how uncomfortable he was when he was not in full control.

Damp, cool air drifted in through the partly opened windows of Michael's red Dodge Dart. The street light's yellow glare was filtered between tiny rain bubbles that had begun to fall on the windshield after we had parked on my block. We had just dropped off another couple who lived in my Forest Hills neighborhood.

During the time that I had sat alone in the night club, I realized that confronting Michael would probably be futile. He would apologize and assure me that such an indiscretion would never happen again ("Jamais, chérie, jamais!"), pleading with sad puppy-dog eyes, and kissing away my protests and reservations.

I wasn't sure that, at nineteen, I would be strong enough to resist Michael at his most charming, but I was petrified that a very painful future with my French amour lay ahead. I instinctively believed that tonight's betrayal was probably not the first, and would certainly not be the last breach of trust. I deeply loved Michael, but I couldn't face a future of peering down dimly lit corridors and being terrified of discovering ugly secrets lurking in dark shadows.

"Michael, we really have to talk," I repeated my earlier imperative.

"Yes, chérie, I could tell that something was on your mind. All evening you have not been yourself."

Only after I saw you kissing Simone!

"That was very perceptive of you. I don't know how else . . ." I folded my hands in my lap to steady my trembling body.

"I know you so well," Michael interjected, sounding smug as he turned to face me.

Not as well as you think!

"Look, Michael," I went on breathlessly, "I've met someone else. I don't know if this will turn into anything—maybe just one date—but while I feel any kind of attraction to him, it's not fair to you if I continue to wear your ring."

My words had spilled out hurriedly, almost slurring one into the other. I was racing to complete my message while I still had the courage.

For once, Michael was stunned into silence. His knuckles turned white as he tightened his grip on the steering wheel.

Of course, the story of another love was a complete fabrication, but Michael seemed to give credence to my "confession." I supposed that habitual liars such as he assumed that other people were not shrewd enough to manipulate the truth.

I took advantage of his shock to pry open his stiff hand and to carefully deposit the ring into it.

"Michael, you're a great guy and I hope we can remain friends," I sobbed. This break-up was proving to be even more difficult to execute than when I had planned it in the night club. Deflating Michael's massive ego, I had concluded, was the only way to ensure that he would be too angry to insinuate his way back into my heart.

In the night club, I had imagined that the tinge of satisfaction of turning the emotional tables on Michael would mitigate some of the agony of ending my engagement. My assumption had been very far from correct. I felt actual physical pain, like my heart was being cut out by Incas in a primitive sacrificial rite.

Before Michael could reply, I quickly exited the car, gently closing the door. I hadn't even paused to open my umbrella, so my tears blended with the quickly increasing showers.

I walked quickly to the glass doors of my apartment building, my heels clicking sharply on the wet pavement. As I entered, I could hear Michael pulling away, car tires screeching loudly on the now rain-soaked street. I was unaware of it at the time, but fate decreed that I would never see him again.

Shuddering, I understood that many sleepless, tear-filled nights, and long days replete with unwelcome, intrusive questions awaited me.

Both in sadness and in cynicism, I wondered just how long it would take for Michael to call Simone.

The hiatus between finals week and the beginning of summer school couldn't have come at a worse time. When I had been dating Michael, holidays and weekends were highly anticipated oases in the monotonous desert of classes. Now, the free time loomed as a dreaded dead zone, empty hours in which there would be nothing to distract me from thoughts of my broken engagement and shattered heart. I seriously doubted that I could ever trust and love another man. There was no respite even in sleep, because Michael's image floated through my dreams, an agonizing reminder of love and betrayal.

I took long, solitary walks over the pedestrian bridge that spanned the Grand Central Parkway and the Van Wyck Expressway and led to Flushing Meadow Park. Once or twice I thought that I recognized Michael ahead of me on the narrow gray path, but when the man turned, he had the face of a stranger. I both mourned and experienced a sense of relief.

I began summer school with my already slender frame ten pounds lighter, and dark circles around my eyes that no pancake make-up could disguise. Happy, pop-song-loving Maddie was gone. She had been replaced by a gaunt, grim, suspicious stranger.

In January, I graduated from Hunter and began my teaching career in a Brooklyn neighborhood that was a mixture of blue-collar workers and new Hispanic immigrants.

Thankfully, the shock of adjusting to the "real school" world—as opposed to the idyllic scenarios described by my education professors—absorbed most of my thoughts and energy. I found that I was actually grateful for the mountainous clerical work—roll books, lesson plans, class lists—that made it easier to block out the happy teachers' room chatter of my newly engaged and recently married colleagues. A great deal of my energy was also consumed with the effort of maintaining a calm, productive, and consistent classroom atmosphere for my pupils, whose home lives were often less than stable.

Almost two years to the day that I had become engaged to Michael, my friend Naomi introduced me to her fiancé's roommate. I met him very reluctantly, mostly to relieve the relentless pressure from family and friends to stop moping and resume dating.

Alex was of medium height, with friendly hazel eyes and dark hair. While he lacked Michael's smooth charm, he was straightforward, reliable, and had a great sense of humor. He was also a whiz in the then-fledgling field of computers.

Alex faced life with common sense softened by kindness. Michael had disliked pets, labeling them "sales"—dirty—but Alex and I shared a love of animals, especially dogs.

I was surprised to find myself looking forward to our dates. Slowly, I began to trust that Alex would not cause me pain. For the first time in almost two years, I was smiling.

Eight months later, my mother was finally able to utilize the catering information that she had gathered during the time that I had been engaged to Michael, and to joyously plan a beautiful wedding that was to be the gateway to a long and happy marriage.

Like the pages of a calendar in an old movie, speedily flipping to show time's passage, the years whizzed by.

I continued to teach until our son was born, and returned after both he and my daughter were old enough to go to and come home from school independently. It seemed almost like one moment that I was fretting about their readiness to remain alone until I arrived at our apartment after work, and in the next instant, that they had both graduated from veterinary school and had gotten married.

2005

Although I could still vividly recall my first blustery February days as a novice teacher, incredibly I was now eligible for retirement. I loved my job as a teacher-trainer in the same Brooklyn school where I had begun my career. However, the realization that "tomorrow is promised to no one" was brought home to me after several of my older colleagues had died almost literally "with the chalk still clutched in their hands." I made the difficult decision to leave while I was still young and healthy enough to enjoy the fruits of my labors.

I began to zestfully partake of my new, leisurely life—working out in a local gym, traveling with Alex, who by now was working part-time, looking forward to the birth of our first grandchild, and attending Teachers Union courses and seminars.

And here I was, listening with sadness to Judith's story as she completed her sordid tale of Michael's duplicity and control, and the way they had impacted her life like a wrecker's ball. She wiped away a tear and leaned over the table, emotionally spent.

Muriel, our instructor, suggested that Judith might wish to teach a course in ballet to retirees who had never had the advantage of lessons. Others, she added, might enjoy brushing up on long forgotten skills. If Judith was interested, she would speak to the union coordinators.

Many of the women in the class responded enthusiastically to Muriel's idea.

"That would be so exciting!"

"I've always wanted to dance!"

"What great exercise!"

Judith lifted her head, smiling slightly. She nodded affirmatively and replied that she would consider teaching a dance class. This week's session was up. Students for the next course to be given in our room waited impatiently in the hall, conversing loudly and staring in through the door's small glass window.

Nevertheless, some members of our group took the time to walk to where Judith stood.

"You're a brave lady."

"Good for you. You finally got rid of him!"

"What a creep!"

In answer to their questions, I heard Judith reply that the last she had heard, Michael had moved in with a French girlfriend. Their sons, now happily married professionals, rarely saw their father. She listened to all their encouraging words, but after that day, she never returned.

Judith's words floated back to me as I slipped out into the gray corridor. The usually slow elevator arrived almost immediately, with flashing red arrow and dinging bell.

Initially, I had planned, over a quiet cup of coffee with Judith, to share my own story of Michael. Then I had thought better of it. Wouldn't it have just rubbed salt in her wounds to learn that someone else had been blessed with clearer foresight, sharper instincts? No, Judith had been hurt enough! I would keep silent.

I walked quickly home along Sixty-Sixth Road, carefully keeping all thoughts of Judith's story out of my mind until I reached my apartment. There, without any distractions, I could reflect on the unsettling information that I just discovered.

After perfunctorily greeting our Airedale mix, Butch, I sat on the comfortable futon in the den and let my emotions wash over me.

Infrequently through the years, I had wondered if Michael had ever settled down, if he had ever met anyone who could inspire him to fidelity. Somehow, I had doubted it, and today's tale had proven me to be correct.

I thought of poor Judith—heart-broken and miserable. I began to tremble, almost vibrate, when I came to the full realization of just how narrowly I had escaped Michael's destructive influence and Judith's bitter fate. There but for the grace of Heaven and my own intuition . . .

I sighed, sober with the knowledge that the road not taken can lead to very dark places.

I looked out of the casement window and saw the setting sun, fiery red with a yellow halo that lent it a three-dimensional, spherical quality.

Then I rose and switched on the radio. Cher's tough, metallic tones pulsated from the pop music station.

"Now I'm strong enough to live without you, strong enough . . ."

I hoped that Judith was also listening and would heed the song's message, but now I had to prepare dinner. Soon Alex would be home.

MARISSA

"You waited, but you really hit the jackpot!" I exclaimed joyously, bending to hug my newly-engaged colleague as my dark hair lightly brushed her cheek. "Marissa, you're an inspiration!"

She really was.

Back then, in the 1960s, any girl who was over twenty-five and still single was considered to be high on the entrance ramp of the expressway to spinsterhood.

The depressing drabness of gray Monday mornings at the Brooklyn elementary school where we taught was somewhat dissipated by suspense as the left hands of single teachers were surreptitiously scrutinized for the presence of newly received, sparkling engagement rings. However, we had all but given up on Marissa Corigliano. She was, after all, twenty-seven or twenty-eight-years old!

Marissa's thick, straight black hair was always perfectly styled in a short page-boy coiffeur that complemented, but never overwhelmed, her lovely, round face. She had been blessed with bright brown eyes, a delicate nose, and a full-lipped mouth, whose shyly proffered smiles revealed even white teeth that could have been featured in dentifrice commercials.

Although Marissa's upper body was a slender size ten and harmonized beautifully with her petite stature, her large hips and thighs exploded unexpectedly from below her waist, and must have required garments of at least a size fourteen.

Marissa cleverly dressed in dark-hued, gently flaring skirts and longer jackets with substantial shoulders. Only on one occasion, when she made the sartorial error of choosing a dress whose bottom portion clung to her overly ample curves, was her unfashionable secret revealed.

Serendipitously, the doors of our third-grade classrooms faced each other. I often stepped across the narrow, dimly lit corridor to consult Marissa. I was twenty-one, unsteadily beginning my career as an educator, and very confused by the myriad forms and puzzling regulations that the Board of Education placed in the paths of neophytes, like obstacles on an athletic field. Marissa's quiet competence and patience was of great help as I gradually learned to understand the bureaucratic lingo and "school speak." However, it was in the "hands on" of my everyday teaching experience that Marissa made such a difference for my pupils and for me.

Only when I had actually started working in the "real school world" could I fully understand just how useless most of my college Educational Methods courses had been, like empty-calorie junk food before a grueling workout, when only a diet rich in high-quality nourishment would be effective in achieving the desired results.

Some of the curriculum guides were also far from helpful. The first November that I taught, the teachers' edition of the children's reader instructed me to regale my class with the tale of how, as a child on Thanksgiving, I had travelled to my grandma's house over an icy brook located in a frozen forest. I shook my head in disbelief and disgust. I had never known my grandparents, and I was raised in Brooklyn, hardly the center of the Great North Woods. What a ludicrous, pretentious conceit!

In contrast to the pompous, self-important pedagogical nonsense with which we were bombarded, practical Marissa emphasized phonics, number skills, book reports, careful work habits, and wall charts which called attention to good behavior and scholastic achievement. I modeled my classroom on her example, and thanks to Marissa's guidance, even the pupils who had been entrusted to me during my novice year of teaching received an excellent education.

I was more outgoing than my quiet, reserved mentor. I chatted frequently with many of our colleagues, but I always shared lunchtimes at the ugly brown Formica tables in the Teachers' Room with Marissa. She was somewhat reticent about her personal life, perhaps because she was a product of her rather insular, self-contained Bensonhurst, Brooklyn, neighborhood. While our friendship did not grow to be deep, and we rarely socialized after hours, there was a caring, affectionate relationship between us. We were like two lily pads in a pond, floating on parallel courses, close, but never quite touching.

I did manage to learn that most of Marissa's free time was spent at home, enjoying domestic activities, in the role of what the Sicilians approvingly label as a "house plant." Indeed, she was most content as the sewing machine whirred, when she was polishing floors and furniture to a brilliant shine, or at the times that the stove was turning out delicious dishes that had been prepared from time-tested recipes. It was a happy day when Marissa brought her creations to work for us to sample! Although she was far too private to vocalize her feelings of loneliness, reading between the lines I understood that she wished that she was expending her housekeeping and culinary efforts on behalf of a husband and family.

In fact, it was Marissa's outstanding homemaking skills and sweet nature that impelled mutual friends to introduce her to her new fiancé, Albert, who had been searching for "an old—fashioned Italian girl."

And now she was finally getting married! Marissa shyly displayed a photo of dark, handsome Albert Scalafia (born in Italy, arrived in the U. S.A. as a teenager), a surgical resident at a prestigious Manhattan hospital. In addition to his other attributes, he possessed a friendly, extroverted personality and, we were blushingly informed, a great sense of humor. His family must have been financially comfortable too, I deduced, because a resident could never have afforded the beautiful, sparkling two-carat diamond that adorned Marissa's left hand.

It was only after our prolonged urging that she reluctantly turned the stone to the front of her finger so that we could admire it. Later she explained to me, "Some of those single girls are older than I am! I wasn't going to show off my ring and depress them. I remember how terrible that can make people feel!" She gave a slight shudder. "I didn't intend to wear it to work at all, but then someone told me that it's very bad luck to *ever* take your engagement ring off before the wedding."

"I'm so thrilled for you!" I exclaimed again, my voice rising with happiness as I embraced Marissa.

"I just hope that you don't have to wait as long as I did, Beth," she replied smiling, as she hugged me back.

The late February announcement of Marissa's engagement happily diverted our thoughts, at least for a time, from the increasingly stressful school schedule—preparations for city-wide tests, parent conferences, report cards—that were beginning to imbue the work atmosphere with tension, like chalk saturating a board eraser. Because of Marissa's good news, most of us could relax enough to smilingly anticipate spring and to visualize the pointy-edged tree branches starting to sprout leaves as emerald blades pierced the brown earth below.

In time, our projections of a balmy future became reality. Spring finally did arrive, and then magical June, the month of Marissa's wedding, floated in on warm breezes.

It was time for the traditional in-school lunchtime bridal shower! In the past, the location for such festivities had always been Jean O'Hanlon's large third-floor room, and this occasion was to be no exception.

The venue for the party had been transformed from a nondescript classroom to a miniature catering hall, which lacked only mirrors and crystal chandeliers. Pink and yellow placemats, streamers, balloons, and a ribbon-trimmed umbrella had been strategically placed by Jean's well-trained pupils. We joked that the children were actually receiving vocational education for a future in the hospitality industry!

Each faculty member brought a gift and a delicious homemade salad, cold-cut platter, or calorie-laden dessert for the celebration. Appetizing, spicy aromas replaced the usual school odors of ink and markers.

Because I was Marissa's closest school friend, I was delegated to lure her to the shower site, using the pretext of an end-term meeting.

I stood behind her as loud, shrill cries of "Surprise!" greeted us as she opened the door of the party room and slowly entered. Flashbulbs lit up the air like fireworks on the Fourth of July.

She stood, facing her smiling colleagues, not really surprised at the expected fete, but more like a queen, who was quietly receiving the good wishes of her subjects. However, she seemed to me to be even more reserved than usual, as she had been during the last several weeks.

As soon as the initial excitement had died down, and the guests were occupied with selecting the delectable foods to fill their pink flower-patterned paper plates, I guided her to a less congested area, in the rear of the classroom.

"Marissa," I spoke softly but distinctly enough to just be heard above the happy din. "What's wrong?"

"Oh, I'm just tired—the last few months—the food, the gown, you know," she answered in her melodic voice, but her deep brown eyes remained sad.

We were standing in front of a language arts bulletin board. Diagonally-posted hundred—per-cent spelling test papers grazed the top of Marissa's dark hair.

"There's nothing else?" I inquired solicitously. Perhaps it was because Marissa understood that I was only interested in her welfare, and that I would never repeat her concerns that, for the first time, she confided in me.

"Oh, all right! It's silly, you'll probably laugh, but it's my grandmother, Costanza."

Marissa had often mentioned this "Nonna," her adored Sicilian grandmother, who lived close to her, and who had taught her to cook and to sew.

"Nonna says that I shouldn't marry Albert, that he has the 'mal occhi,' the evil eye. Such nonsense!"[1]

She gave a tiny laugh, but I could tell by the slight tremor in her voice as she recounted the weird, shocking warning that it had saddened and disturbed her.

"That's really crazy and cruel," I thought, "to ruin her joy after she's waited so long." But how could I tell Marissa that her darling Nonna was a superstitious, medieval-thinking nut? Yet, I felt impelled to extend some words of comfort.

"She loves you so much that she's overprotective. No guy would be good enough," I suggested, patting her arm.

"You know," Marissa said slowly, nodding her head, "You're probably right." Her sweet smile began to return, and her eyes started to regain some of their usual brightness.

Later, my words would come back to haunt me.

No members of the faculty or administration were invited to the wedding that Marissa had so carefully planned.

"I would feel terrible if people came to the church, and I couldn't invite them to the reception in the restaurant after, but my Mom and I just can't afford it." Marissa shook her head. "I'll really miss everyone from work, especially you, Beth, but with us the bride pays for everything, and Albert and I both have large families. I'm so sorry."

Mrs. Corigliano, a widow, lived on a barely adequate pension that she supplemented with a part-time job working in a bakery. Marissa also had limited financial resources, because at that time teachers earned little more than unskilled office workers, so a large, catering hall wedding and its attendant expenses was obviously out of the question.

"Don't worry, I'll be there in spirit, and you can show me the pictures later. Just be happy!" I squeezed her hand.

The new couple had decided that after their June marriage, Marissa would work only through the fall semester, until Albert had completed his residency. I knew how much the new bride loved children, so I assumed that after Marissa had left her teaching job she would attempt to start a family.

Autumn leaves may have been tumbling down, but Marissa's weight was quickly rising. She described the delicious, irresistible meals that she was preparing nightly, and I was sure that the tempting pasta dishes were the cause of the increasing poundage that was becoming more apparent with each day that passed. However, I wrote down the recipes for some of the more remarkable meals, despite their high caloric content. I was seriously dating Ben, a good-humored teddy-bear-like engineer, whom my cousin had introduced me to over the summer, and I projected that I might soon feel the need to impress him with my culinary skills.

Now, no amount of camouflage dressing could disguise Marissa's steadily expanding figure. I could only hope that Albert had a fondness for full-figured, Rubenesque type women.

Marissa left on a blustery, snowy day at the end of January during my second year of teaching. I missed my mentor and lunch companion, and her pupils missed her quiet, structured teaching style, especially when Marissa was replaced with a ditzy, disorganized older lady whose slovenly appearance was reflected in her classroom management style.

In the weeks following Marissa's departure, we spoke on the telephone from time to time. Surprisingly, she suggested that we meet in the city for drinks with "the guys." I was delighted that marriage seemed to be making her more extroverted, and that she was reaching out to me, but before each eagerly awaited reunion, our plans were unfortunately disrupted.

Once, together with many of my pupils, I contracted a debilitating stomach virus from my student Jimmy shortly after he was stricken with this miserable affliction.

"You said that you were already very ill at home, so why did you come to school?" I had demanded of the pale, periodically vomiting eight-year-old, who, only with difficulty, could raise his head to answer.

"My mother had to go to my aunt's," the poor, feverish child had replied almost inaudibly.

Three later dates were cancelled at the very last minute because Albert was suddenly put on emergency duty. After, I wondered just how legitimate those assignments had been.

Towards the end of March, I called Marissa to share joyous news—I was engaged to Ben, and we were planning an August wedding.

"Oh, Beth, I'm so happy for you," she gushed into the phone with an exuberance that was a departure from her usual calm, unruffled manner of speaking.

"And even if we can't manage to get together now, especially with the holidays coming and all, I expect to see you when they 'trick' me into Jean's room for a surprise shower!" I joked.

"I wouldn't miss it for the world!" Marissa assured me.

My June shower was not, after all, at Jean's. Gilda Giordano had volunteered her classroom for the party, so I really was somewhat surprised, if not completely shocked. However, I was prepared enough to be wearing a floaty, fuchsia skirt and matching top, as I had dressed up "just in case" for the last several days.

Once again, as at Marissa's celebration, the rainbow colors of the decorations and beautifully wrapped gifts echoed the hues of the flowers that bloomed in the small yards of the school's shabby neighborhood. Savory aromas and happy chatter filled the air. Exploding flashbulbs assured that the occasion would be immortalized on film. The only missing component was the highly anticipated presence of Marissa.

I was disappointed and concerned. Could her new red Dodge Dart, despite its sterling reputation, have had mechanical problems? Perhaps her mother had been taken ill? But then wouldn't Marissa have notified the school? Her absence threw a color-leaching pall over the pastel-hued shower, but I attempted to affect a joyous, celebratory air as I joked and laughed with my colleagues. After all, while these parties were labors of love, they still involved a lot of planning and hard work, and I certainly didn't wish to appear unhappy or ungrateful.

At the festivities' end, I was loaded down with gifts. It was time for me to pick up my class, so, reluctantly (maybe Marissa might still arrive?), I took my leave and began to make my way downstairs to the pupils' lunchroom. I didn't get very far. Unexpectedly, I was intercepted in the hall by the principal, Mr. Sidney Clemens. Initially, I assumed that "Old

Gray"—gray hair, gray complexion, gray personality—was attempting to extend congratulations in his dry, unemotional fashion.

He began slowly. "Mrs. Navarro (the school secretary) suggested that we wait until after your shower to tell you."

"Tell me what?" I asked, a note of apprehension creeping into my voice as it rose slightly on the word "what."

"Well, they found Marissa," he continued, fiddling with his gray and black tie.

"Found her? Why, was she lost? That's impossible! She drove here so many times!" I asked, confused.

"No, no. Her sister called and said that Marissa just didn't wake up this morning. They think that she had a stroke. You know how heavy she'd gotten. Her husband said that last night she complained of a very severe headache. He begged her to let him take her to the emergency room, but she refused. She just took some aspirin and went to bed. According to the sister, Mrs. Antonelli, she had been very excited about coming to your shower. She had a gift all wrapped and ready to take to you today."

My eyes burned. I leaned back heavily against a close-by, windowless classroom door.

"Oh, poor Marissa . . . oh, how terrible!" I gasped. I was trembling from head to toe.

Was it my imagination, or did even the imperturbable Mr. Clemens look upset? He shook his head with incredulity as he reached out to steady the pile of presents that teetered precariously in my now very unsteady arms.

"I guess they'll call about the wake," I stammered. Even as I spoke, my voice sounded distant, and I felt that the rather dispassionate statement was being articulated by another, less involved person. After, I could only surmise that I was so stunned by Marissa's death that I was on emotional auto-pilot.

"Yes, Mrs. Antonelli said that they would notify us, but there was some problem. I don't know exactly what it was."

Through my grief I thought, *What kind of problem could there possibly be?*

That afternoon, I found it very difficult to focus on teaching. Every time my classroom door opened, I involuntarily looked over at the room that had been Marissa's. Immediately, I averted my eyes so that my pupils would not see that I was furiously fighting back tears.

The next morning, I was awakened by the pale lemon bars of sunlight that streamed under the blinds. The clock on the night table next to me showed that it was almost six-thirty. My first thoughts were of Ben. Soon we'd be married!

Then, as if someone had peeled back the bedcovers and splashed icy water on my still half—asleep body, I remembered Marissa, and her unimaginable death that had shocked everyone, like a noisy explosion in a hushed library. Immediately, my feelings of pre-wedding happiness disappeared, transformed into vapor on the warm June air.

Slowly, I walked into the kitchen and turned on the radio at low volume, so as not to awaken my parents, who were enjoying the last twenty minutes of slumber before they, too, would have to rise to prepare for their work day. Every morning I listened to the headlines on the half hour as I filled the shiny copper kettle.

The jarring notes that signaled a breaking news story drowned out the sound of the water as it splashed out of the faucet.

"A New York physician is described as a person of interest in the death of his wife." The announcer spoke with the proper combination of urgency and gravity.

I had never been psychic, but somehow, in that instant, I knew what was to follow.

"Dr. Albert Scalafia is in police custody. He is being held for questioning (he was later charged and convicted) in the death of his wife, Marissa. A spokesman for law enforcement declined to give any further details at this time."

I staggered against the granite counter in dismay. My loud cries of disbelief and horror echoed throughout our apartment and sent my unceremoniously awakened, startled parents racing to my side with panic-driven steps.

As the days progressed, more horrendous details emerged.

Very soon after he had discovered his wife's body, Albert had voiced a sudden, bizarre wish for Marissa to be summarily cremated. However, a sharp-eyed detective had, almost immediately, spied a suspicious puncture mark that was nearly hidden between the two larger toes of

Marissa's left foot. Despite Albert's strenuous objections to an autopsy, and his authoritatively stated medical opinion that "the anticipation of a celebration in her former place of employment spiked a dangerous rise in blood pressure that caused a massive stroke," a post-mortem examination *was* performed. Marissa's blood was found to contain several times the amount of Demerol that would constitute a normal dose.

Judicious questioning of hospital personnel revealed that, for the last six months, Albert had been conducting an affair with a young, blond surgical nurse, and that he was deeply involved with her.

"We all knew something was going on between those two," an anonymous nurse was later quoted as saying. "The looks, the hugs and hand holding when they thought nobody was looking. Oh yes, we knew that they were in love, but we never thought that Dr. Scalafia would hurt his wife!"

Albert had to have understood that Marissa would never—for religious and emotional reasons—have agreed to a divorce.

It sent chills through me when I learned how close the murderous physician had come to getting away with his unspeakable crime. He had attempted to pull the wool over the Corigliano family's eyes as he played the tearful, inconsolable husband. Albert had attempted to disguise his horrendous deed in the cloak of professionalism and ostensible devotion in the same fashion that Marissa had sought to hide her body flaws in cleverly chosen outfits.

Had Marissa been aware of the threat to her marriage, and had her last days been filled with anxiety and sadness, or had she been blissfully unaware of sinister vibes from her evil-eyed husband before he committed the ultimate betrayal? Because of Marissa's very private character, the question could never be answered with certainty.

Right now, there was only grief for those of us who had loved and cared for her, and lessons to be learned.

Some of the older, single teachers had been bitterly envious of Marissa's "good fortune" in "marrying so well." Perhaps this tragedy would teach those with open hearts and minds to be grateful for their immediate blessings, and to savor the small joys of everyday living without constantly comparing their circumstances with those of their peers.

Others, more introspective, might also come to understand that situations are not always as they appear on the surface, and that some people—like old grandmothers—have an incredible gift for seeing beyond the external, and into the dark crevices of the human soul.

SABBATH ELIXIR—
A WHIMSICAL TALE

Who knows what secrets lurk just beneath the most nondescript surfaces,
and what mystery surrounds even the most forthright-appearing actions?

Outwardly, the rectangular beige *shul* (synagogue) was not conspicuous
on the tree-lined streets of Forest Hills, where almost every thoroughfare
could boast of at least one Jewish house of worship. The distinctiveness of
the appropriately named Congregation *Shomrei Zakainim* (Guardians of
the Aged) lay not in its architecture, but in its membership.

The original synagogue had been founded in 1939 by Jews who had
fled Nazi Germany and arrived in Washington Heights, in the borough
of Manhattan. Through the years, gratitude for their escape was reflected
in hymns of praise and thanksgiving to the Almighty, perhaps even
more heartfelt than those of many other congregations. The mourners'
prayers heard in *Shomrei Zakainim* were especially poignant, as memories
of family and friends who had been consumed by the Holocaust were
recalled and honored.

After most of the members had moved to Forest Hills, Queens, in
the seventies, the *shul* followed, buying still relatively inexpensive land
and erecting an attractive but unremarkable edifice. The interior followed
the modest example of the exterior and featured beige walls and brown
pews. This rather austere décor was enlivened only by a large needlepoint
tapestry that was based on a colorful Chagall window. Somehow, its vivid
blues, brilliant reds, and intense gold seemed oddly out of place, like
flower tattoos on a great-grandmother.

What made the congregation noteworthy, then, was not the
elegance of its structure, nor the wealth of its members—it was their
advanced ages. While a few illnesses and deaths did occur, overall, the

people enjoyed levels of vigor and longevity that were nothing short of miraculous.

President Ben Behrmann, a wiry retired tool-and-die maker, originally from Berlin, was a feisty 97-year-old who enlivened board meetings with his strong opinions (always fiscally conservative) and sharp intellect. He still chafed at the thought of the annual fund-raising dinner being held in an outside catering facility, rather than in the *shul's* unpretentious social hall. When he was not involved in the congregation's workings and politics, he and his elegant, well-coiffed 87-year-old wife, Hannalore, took *spaziers* (strolls), on upscale Austin Street, where they enjoyed greeting neighbors and *Shomrei Zakainim* members.

Ninety-year-old sisterhood president Hildegard Loewenstein, a retired bookkeeper who had been born in Frankfurt-am-Main, ran the surprisingly lucrative yearly bazaars. Her nearly six-foot presence deterred even the boldest patron from bargaining when, shaking her gray head, she would declare in her no-nonsense manner, "Take it or leef it!"

The well-priced item would usually be quickly snatched up.

Bazaar security was provided by the *Shomrei Zakainim* "toughs," who were male members in their eighties and nineties. What was wonderful was not the protection they provided but, as they patrolled the crowded aisles, that these geriatric guardsmen perceived themselves to be threats to potential shoplifters.

Ninety-two-year-old Katherine Ehrlich, a native of Hamburg, wore her hair in a practical "wash and wear" bob. Her stylist often commented on the fact that Katherine had an amazingly insignificant amount of gray for a woman of her age.

Katherine, a widow, ran the spotless *Shomrei Zakainim* kitchen, where she prepared the weekly *kiddush* (collation after services), usually unassisted. When the *shul's* social hall was rented out for parties or luncheons, she very grudgingly granted the caterer access to her immaculate domain.

The hearts and souls of most synagogues are their rabbis, and that was certainly the case with *Shomrei Zakainim*. Rabbi Guttmann had fled Frankfurt in 1938 and arrived, together with his family, in Washington Heights as a scholarly 15-year-old. He was learned in both Jewish and secular studies. A slight, bearded man with penetrating but kindly blue eyes, he and his wife could often be found visiting the ill or delivering home-cooked meals to shut-ins, members and nonmembers alike.

No needy person ever left the *shul* with empty pockets, and no lonely congregant ever went without invitations for holiday dinners. Strict in his own devotion to religious laws, Rabbi Guttmann was nonjudgmental and forgiving of others.

Of course, some middle-aged people joined from time to time, to the delight of the seniors. For several months, a husband and wife in their fifties who had recently become part of the congregation were referred to as "the new young couple."

Rabbi Guttmann encouraged many of the neighborhood's new Russian immigrants to be part of the synagogue family when he instituted services in their native tongue and a Hebrew school geared to their children's needs. Jews from such diverse places as Morocco, India, Hungary, and the United States were made to feel welcome as well. And so the congregation slowly grew, despite the fact that many of the offspring of the *shul's* members elected to buy homes on "the island" or in New Jersey, where the housing dollar could be stretched much farther.

Rebecca Wiseman was one excited 12-year-old! Her February *bat mitzvah* (religious coming-of-age ceremony for girls) was to be held in the *Shomrei Zakainim* social hall. Even if they were not *shul* members, the hall was a popular choice with many of Rebecca's friends and their parents. The girls liked the neutral beige walls and carpeting that blended with any color decorations; the parents favored the inexpensive rental fee. A female disc jockey had been engaged to play tapes of lively tunes that were performed by popular Chasidic artists. Katz caterers had been hired to serve a delicious and festive dairy meal, the preferred repast of bat mitzvah celebrations.

Early on the morning of the party, Manny Katz arrived with his two assistants, Boris Gorishvili and Jimmy Armstrong. Boris, a newcomer from Georgia in the former Soviet Union, aspired to eventually open his own catering service to meet the needs of his growing community. Jimmy just aspired to support himself honestly. Every time 19-year—old Jimmy heard a radio or TV segment urging people to get flu shots, he just shook his blond, curly-haired head. Having the flu had probably saved his life.

After dropping out of Lane High School, Jimmy had earned cash by bodega break-ins, a not uncommon occupation in his East New York neighborhood. He was usually joined by his buddy from Brooklyn's

Public School 108, Willie Green. The boys had bonded in the fourth grade because of a shared love of baseball cards.

Soon after they had met, during Brotherhood Week, Jimmy had proudly declared, "I'm white, he's black, and we get along great!" A smart-aleck teacher had wisecracked, "Yeah, you're both equal-opportunity pains in the neck!" The boys had collapsed with laughter, their arms still around one another.

Now they had a new, if less wholesome, common interest. They would wait until two or three o'clock in the morning and quietly (thanks to Jimmy's lock-picking prowess) break into a targeted store. Several shopkeepers were known to leave modest amounts of cash in registers or "hidden" in obvious places to prevent costly vandalism by frustrated thieves. On occasion, the boys also "liberated" relatively more expensive items—mostly canned goods—and resold them at discount prices in a scaled-down, East New York version of "it fell off the truck." They figured that they had a good thing going—not as lucrative as robbing stores that were open, but certainly not as dangerous.

Willie's and Jimmy's single mothers were too involved in the day-to-day problems of maintaining their households to really become concerned with their sons' less than exemplary nocturnal activities. As long as their boys didn't appear to be involved with drugs, the leprosy that rotted the fabric of their Brooklyn environment, the moms figured that Jimmy and Willie were just experiencing a rite of passage common to their shabby neighborhood. Best of all, because their sons had an outside source of revenue, the mothers were not pestered for spending cash by their offspring.

"Just don't let the cops catch you and throw your sorry behinds in jail, because I won't be able do a damn thing to help you!" Jimmy's mother yelled, shaking her index finger and her brassy blond head simultaneously at her son and his best friend. Then she raced out of the cramped apartment's door. She could not be late for her part-time job at a Macy's cosmetics counter in the Queens Center mall.

One Wednesday in the September before the Wiseman *bat mitzvah*, Willie had arranged with Jimmy to hit the small grocery store on Linwood and Arlington. The plan was to meet at ten on Monday night in the nearby schoolyard, hang out under the 1895 constructed P.S. 108's shadowy gables, and later "pull the job."

As he watched cartoons on television Monday afternoon, Jimmy experienced an unfamiliar, annoying tickle in his throat. By late evening, he was inundated simultaneously with chills and fiery-hot flushes, like a junkie in withdrawal. Every bone in his body was being tortured with pounding, incessant pains as he twisted uncomfortably under the bedcovers. Incredibly, even his eyelids hurt.

Around eleven, Willie had dropped by to find out why his co-conspirator hadn't made an appearance.

Jimmy had moaned, "Don't go without me. You'll see, I'll be okay tomorrow."

However, one look at Jimmy's pale, sweaty face and trembling body had convinced Willie that he would be partner-less, and thus also cashless, for several days—just now, just now, when he had finally managed to score a date with the cute and sassy LaTonya Stokes!

"Get better, man. See you," he had mumbled as he left the small, uncarpeted bedroom. He decided to do what seemed to be a fairly simple job alone.

The following morning Jimmy's condition hadn't improved, but what took his breath away wasn't the effects of the flu, but the news his distraught mother had screamed out as she ran to his bedside as her freshly dyed hair flew in every direction, her tears already eroding her heavily applied make-up.

"Willie, he got shot! He's dead! The bodega guy got him!"

Jimmy slumped back on his pillow, his eyes burning. Only a few hours ago, Willie had stood right in front of him talking, his lanky body draped over the rickety second-hand maple chest of drawers. Now he would never see his best friend again.

Although his cognitive processes were fuzzy with fever and grief, Jimmy was still sharp enough to recognize how close he himself had come to being killed. He began to see Willie's death as a warning and a sign that he should eschew a life of crime and try to obtain legitimate employment.

Shortly after Jimmy finally recovered from the flu, a neighbor casually mentioned that she was leaving her job at Katz's Catering to return to her family in Puerto Rico. Jimmy had immediately applied for the newly vacated position and was hired on a trial basis.

Surprisingly, Jimmy discovered that he was gifted with a very real talent for the food service industry. His skills with lock-picking tools adapted easily to the carving knife and pastry tube, like the transference of literary aptitude from one language to another. His presentations were so artistic, with beautifully sculpted fruit designs and lovely radish roses, that he soon became a valued member of the "Katz Team."

Boris and Jimmy put the finishing touches on the cantaloupe and honeydew platter (cut edges down to create more uniform appeal) for Rebecca's *bat mitzvah* reception. They quickly filled in the spaces with red and green grapes, and then turned their attentions to the crudités platter. Soon after he started to arrange the julienned carrots, yellow squash, and cucumbers around a glass dish of Thousand Island dressing, Boris excused himself and stepped outside to use his cell phone—something about his son's *yeshiva* (Jewish religious school).

Jimmy's glance fell on a locked cabinet that he had noticed on previous visits. He wondered if some rich old coot had hidden money inside. It certainly was worth checking out and, Jimmy rationalized, just satisfying his curiosity wasn't really dishonest

Quickly, with the fruit knife grasped between his delicate fingers, he opened the padlock so dexterously that it wasn't even scratched.

Bummer! All that he found was a tall green bottle with a very long, thin neck and grape-cluster designs etched all around it. It was filled with a liquid that Jimmy decided could easily be wine. An eye-dropper had been placed next to the glass vessel. When he unscrewed the bottle's tightly fastened cap, a tantalizing, spicy aroma wafted gently to his nostrils. Jimmy tilted the bottle slightly and took a small, tentative sip, followed by a more robust gulp.

The red liquid had a wonderfully rich, nutty-sweet flavor, unlike anything he had ever tasted. A tremendous surge of energy and well-being encompassed him, and the depression that he still felt over Willie's death seemed to magically lift. Good stuff! It was extremely difficult for Jimmy to force himself to stop imbibing this wonderful beverage, but he knew that discovery of "drinking on the job" would probably cause immediate dismissal from his relatively well-compensated and enjoyable employment. Besides, he realized that he had to work very quickly before

Boris returned, to implement the plan that was already forming in his head.

Without replacing the bottle on its shelf, Jimmy swiftly closed the cabinet door and clipped the lock back into place. After his first sip of the delicious nectar, he had immediately decided against returning the green glass container to its original place. Suppose its owner reclaimed it, and it was never available again? He would have loved to have taken this extraordinary decanter home, but it was much too large to conceal.

The next best thing, Jimmy reasoned, was to keep it where he would be guaranteed its exclusive use—like the wine cellars of the rich and famous which were shown so often on the television.

By mounting the yellow kitchen stepstool, he reached the top shelf of the paper goods closet. With a mighty stretch of his five-foot-four body that threatened to separate his midsection from his faded work jeans, he secreted the bottle behind several piles of Styrofoam coffee cups, which almost completely obstructed it from view.

When Boris returned, the Georgian was amazed to see the crudités completed, and the fish platter well underway as Jimmy placed rolled slices of lox around a whitefish that he had already filleted.

"You real fast today!" the big Russian complimented the beaming Jimmy.

The following Friday morning, Katherine was once again happily in charge of the *shul* kitchen. She arranged the thinly cut (no need to waste) slices of honey and sponge cake on aluminum platters for the next day's *kiddush*. The trays were carefully covered with Saran Wrap and placed in the huge stainless-steel refrigerator. Katherine then took her key and unlocked the cabinet that had previously held the large bottle of liquid that had so captivated Jimmy, and which was extremely essential in the preparation of the wine and grape juice. The dropper lay alone on the shelf, next to the space that had formerly been occupied by its glass container companion.

Katherine stood frozen. The color drained out of her cheeks, and her petite form staggered against the pristine counter. To ensure that she had correctly observed the shelf's empty condition, she quickly pulled her glasses from her small beige purse. When she shakily put them on, her eyes, already wide with horror, were magnified to an unbelievable size.

"Vot happen?" she gasped aloud. "Ver is the bottle?"

She carefully searched the kitchen, but her hunt was in vain. With a heavy heart, she finished readying the *kiddush.*

After only a fortnight, a marked difference in the congregation could be observed. Eighty—and ninety-year—old members who, just a few short weeks before had been astonishingly limber, were suffering from severe attacks of arthritis. Nearly everyone was reporting greater difficulty in deciphering the smaller print of the *Aufbau* (A German-Jewish weekly newspaper).

For her entire life, Mrs. Erna Baumgartner had functioned very well without glasses, but now, with her vision suddenly impaired, the lively 88-eight-year-old tripped over a rug that she had owned for nearly thirty years, badly twisting her ankle.

Even though he had reached the age of ninety-four, Mr. Erik Rosenhaus had always maintained an unblemished driving record, without even a parking ticket to mar it. He often made the difficult trip over the heavily traveled Triboro Bridge to visit family members who still remained in Washington Heights.

However, in the last week, his remarkable reflexes were somehow diminished, and he was involved in a fender-bender with a UPS truck on hilly Fort Washington Avenue, a busy thoroughfare in "the Heights."

Throughout the years, Mrs. Lotte Kronheim, a retired milliner, had enjoyed baking her specialty, *apfel schalet* (apple pudding), for family and friends to enjoy. But soon after the green bottle's disappearance, when her grandchildren eagerly sampled the beloved sweet treat, their noses wrinkled in spontaneous shock and revulsion. An inappropriate foreign flavor had assaulted their taste buds like a mugger hitting an unsuspecting victim over the head.

It was subsequently revealed that chubby 95-year-old Lotte, in a never-before—experienced state of confusion, had replaced the recipe's required cup-and-a-half of sugar with the same measure of salt.

Newly purchased canes and walkers were much in evidence. Acquaintances of many years suddenly had trouble recalling their friends' names. *Gemuetlich* (pleasant) conversations were replaced by tales of medical woes. Indeed, complaining was suddenly being raised to an art form, and everyone's philosophy seemed to be "I kvetch, therefore I am."

To make matters worse, Passover, a festive holiday involving heavy and thorough cleaning, was fast approaching.

In accordance with Jewish law, homes as well as the synagogue had to be scoured and searched to remove any traces of bread.

Three weeks before the holiday, Vadim, the tall, husky Russian *shul* custodian, climbed slowly and wearily up the yellow stepstool with a flashlight clutched in his hand to check the very top shelves of the storage closet.

"A ridiculous task!" he thought in disgust. "Who puts *chometz* (unleavened food products) with paper goods? *Sumashedshi* (Crazy)!"

Suddenly, as he grudgingly searched the top shelf, a beam from his flashlight was reflected by the tall neck of a bottle, placed in a dark corner at the very rear, that loomed over the cups like a skyscraper towering over a city.

Could it be? Was this the decanter that Katherine kept talking about and searching for? He fervently hoped that it was. She would certainly be delighted and probably, at least for a little while, stop nagging him.

Quickly he shoved aside the Styrofoam products to carefully remove the decanter and to very gingerly place it on the counter below.

When Vadim called Katherine to give her the news, she surprised him by immediately walking over to examine his find. Her home was located at least ten blocks away, and the late March weather was showery, windy, and chilly—no day for a 92-year-old to be out, the custodian thought.

As Katherine smilingly beheld the treasured vessel, joy suffused her delicately wrinkled face. Fortunately, the decanter's contents had been only slightly diminished by Jimmy's two subsequent visits and furtive, rushed samplings.

The bottle would not be jeopardized again! From that day forward, it was kept in Katherine's spotless apartment. Each week, she wheeled it to the *shul* in her shopping cart, which boasted a protective, heavy-duty plaid liner. Once she arrived, Katherine added several drops of the decanter's contents to the wine and grape juice that was to be served at the next day's *kiddush*.

During his next catering assignment, Jimmy slumped in disappointment at not finding his prized beverage. As he disconsolately hulled strawberries, he began to see the disappearance of the bottle as yet another sign—especially as it had been given in a house of worship—that honesty would indeed be the best policy to follow for the rest of his life.

That very day, Jimmy enrolled in a training program for gourmet chefs, which was to be given at a prestigious Manhattan culinary school.

Immediately after the recovery of the green decanter, Katherine excitedly called the congregation to be sure to attend a special *kiddush* on Saturday. The reason for the unusual, lavish spread was never given. Although many of the members were not up to snuff, the fine weather on that day encouraged most people to attend services. The ladies dressed in their best beige suits in honor of the festive meal.

Oddly, within about two-and-a-half weeks and just in time for Passover, the "Festival of Redemption," everyone began to appear more like their old selves. Gradually, walkers, canes, and even wheelchairs were discarded, and aches and pains subsided. Once again, even the small print in the *Aufbau* became intelligible.

Serendipitously, Mr. Rosenhaus found that his remarkable reflexes had been restored. He proudly resumed the drives to Washington Heights that had so enriched his life and the lives of his relatives.

Mrs. Kronheim was thrilled that her exceptional concentration had returned. She was able to follow exactly the instructions of heirloom recipes, as in the past, and to create delicious baked goods, including special Passover confections.

Slowly, circumstances returned to normal in the congregation that was unremarkable, except for the age and health of its members.

GARDEN SANCTUARY

The large silver truck careens off the exit ramp from the FDR. Its wheels make contact with the pavement of 34th Street, causing a thunderous crash, a boom louder than any bass drum could ever achieve.

Following closely in the truck's wake come several autos, creating only a few decibels less racket as they maneuver wildly, like cars in an amusement park attraction.

As they turn onto First Avenue, the vehicles, their exhaust pipes' discharge further thickening the already polluted air, join the cacophony of blaring horns, screeching brakes, and throbbing sirens—the discordant concert of New York traffic.

Unbelievably, just a few feet away from the nerve-jangling city sounds lies an island of beauty and serenity—the large, enclosed garden of NYU's Rusk Rehabilitation Center.

Today, the garden is providing me with a peaceful sanctuary as I await the time of a medical check-up.

As I age, even routine exams cause a certain level of anxiety—a flashback to the era of college midterms, with the accompanying slightly quickened breath, and hands that are just a bit colder than normal.

So far, the garden's unpublicized reputation allows unrestricted access to the small number of New Yorkers who are aware of its existence. I am fortunate to be among those select few.

Here, aisles are lined with vari-sized terra-cotta-potted plants that are crowded together like SRO patrons at a much-acclaimed opera. The plants' leaves—spiky or gently rounded, chartreuse, hunter, or fuchsia-edged—reach toward the angled roof, their tropism similar to the stretches of students in a Pilates class.

As the sun filters in, it silhouettes the greenhouse's glass panels and the plants' shapes on the gray concrete floor. From time to time, the foliage sways in the delicate, fan-induced breeze. Those plants gifted with red, orange, or pink flowers seem to proudly proffer their blossoms. "Look at me! Look at me!"

Parrots, cockatiels, and parakeets inhabit large white cages that have been strategically placed amidst the greenery to evoke the image of a rainforest. Loud chirping rings out and is heard over the serene WQXR music that almost waltzes in on sunbeams. The bright blues, yellows, whites and grays of the birds' plumage seem to virtually glow in the warm air that is thick with the musky-sweet aroma of well-cared-for vegetation.

From time to time, a wheelchair-bound patient will be pushed through the garden, sometimes rising to pat the head of the friendly cockatoo, Bobby, and to earn an approving smile from the therapist.

Suddenly the clamorous outside world intrudes! A deliveryman pushes a dolly of cardboard-boxed plants past the entrance and the fishpond. He is clad in a glaring, neon lime shirt and shouts into a cell phone as he progresses to the workroom that is at the garden's rear.

"He'd better do the right thing! He's on parole, and if he messes up, he goes right back to jail, big time!" He automatically waves one hand to emphasize his point, a gesture that cannot possibly be appreciated by the unseeing caller.

I shudder as if his high-volume conversation has disturbed a sacred place. The birds chirp more loudly, more quickly.

A gray-haired woman in a too-bright orange pantsuit (with hideously coordinating knapsack) approaches the front of each of the ten cages. She leans forward at every stop and shrieks, "Hello, hello, HELLOOO!" in a high-pitched voice that threatens to shatter the greenhouse's glass. The birds stare, momentarily shocked into silence.

Small, dark wild birds from the stunted, concrete-constricted First Avenue trees often fly in through open hospital doors. They flit and dart under the cages, searching for fallen crumbs and seeds. Are these outsiders like callers on Visiting Day at Riker's Island Prison, or are they more akin to the homeless, jealously staring up at apartment dwellers, who, illuminated by soft lamplight, gaze out of their cozy residences?

Finally, the Philistine invaders retreat. The deliveryman pushes an empty dolly. This time, his coarse phone conversation is punctuated by obscenities as he progresses towards the door.

As she exits, a smile still fixed on her face, the "orange woman" ridiculously continues to attempt her shrill calls to the now-indifferent birds.

At last, the only remaining sounds are the music, soft chirping, and the bubbling of the fish pond as its copper-gold residents glide through sage waters.

Once again at peace, I relax in my reclaimed oasis.

*   *   *   *   *   *   *   *   *

A sad postscript—The Glass Garden was totally destroyed by Hurricane Sandy in October of 2013.

The Secret Monarch

While the moon still glows in the black pre-dawn sky,
I descend to my subterranean kingdom,
Where mechanized subjects await my bidding,
Their Cyclops eyes embedded in stainless steel bodies.
I reign supreme, in splendor and in solitude,
With no plebeian neighbors to interfere.
In the Linoleum-floored "throne room," mine alone,
At this early time, secluded as a deep dungeon.
A privileged ruler's choice: hot, warm, or cold water?
Vigorous, permanent press, or gentle cycle?
Royal blue detergent, morphing into
The pure white of ermine-trimmed regalia.
Machines whir, singing imagined paeans of tribute,
To my ears, acknowledgment of my dominion,
As they strive to fulfill imperial commands.
After, other drones channel tropical heat
Evaporating moisture like a summer drought
Clothes now dry as a sirocco-parched emirate.
My hand, extended in a gesture of grace,
Not elegantly yielding a jeweled scepter
But in wry exchange, a pink plastic clothes hanger,
Finally, my stately robes pristine and fragrant,
I wave farewell, like a condescending noble,
To a crowd of adoring commoners.
I take leave of my fantasy domain,
Where pretending can lighten an odious chore,
And time rockets by on flights of fancy.
I'll renew my sovereignty next week, as
The 6 AM Queen of the building laundry room!

A SMALL WEDDING

1990

"Nancy, I didn't know that you were such a nosher!" My petite sister Sonya laughed, tossing her curly auburn hair as she looked up at my daughter. Sonya was referring to the old folk belief that if a girl was an inveterate in-between-meal nibbler, it would surely rain on her wedding day.

And now it was indeed raining—not a hard, soaking shower, but tiny drops like frosty effervescent bubbles of seltzer were falling copiously around us. We had just left the family Buick after struggling to simultaneously open our umbrellas and gain our footing on the pavement, where the overhead glow of the street lights was reflected on the moisture-laden concrete. Fortunately, my husband, who served as our driver, had spied a parking space only about half a block away from the Forest Hills Jewish Center.

This temple, in which the ceremony was to be held, loomed over Queens Boulevard like a large, seemingly gray boulder which blended into the evening's foggy darkness. Only when one came close to the entrance's torch-shaped lights was it apparent that the building was not gray after all, but that it was constructed of beautifully golden-highlighted Jerusalem stone.

Nancy was to be married before a small group of family and very close friends in the rabbi's wood-paneled study. She had never favored the lavish weddings—costly gown, smorgasbord, dinner, and Viennese dessert table—that were so popular with her peers. Other mothers had joked how lucky I was to avoid the headaches and expenses of a large affair. It would, they assured me, be much easier to arrange the small restaurant reception that Nancy had selected to celebrate her nuptials. I had laughingly agreed, but in my heart I would have loved to see my beautiful, green-eyed Nancy in full bridal regalia. Still, it was her wedding, and I would never have interfered with her wishes. I could well understand how quiet, shy Nancy would hate being the focus of everyone's attention. She had always shunned the limelight.

When my daughter had been about ten years old and still in elementary school, the mother of one of her classmates who was having difficulty with math telephoned me. This woman thanked me profusely for the time Nancy took to tutor her daughter during recess and lunch.

I was quite surprised. Nancy had never mentioned helping Lily.

When I complimented her that night for her unselfishness, embarrassed and blushing, she had replied, "I feel sorry for her. Some of the kids laugh when she makes mistakes."

I had smiled. "Maybe you'll be a teacher, like me."

My comment had been prophetic. Eleven years later, Nancy graduated from Queens College with a Bachelor's degree in education.

More recollections of Nancy flashed through my mind.

Seven years prior to Nancy's wedding day, on a family trip to California, we had stumbled upon a vegetarian kosher Chinese restaurant. It featured delicious mock meats, chicken, and fish served in a clean but unadorned setting that was unremarkable except for the pungent, appetizing odors that greeted patrons.

Suddenly Nancy had risen quickly from the table, her eyes fixed on a small, bare window opposite her chair. She had exclaimed in delight, "Look at what I found!"

Slightly below the level of the dining room, almost hidden from view, lay a tiny, perfect Asian garden with Hunter-green bushes, bonsai trees, and delicate pink flowers. A high, narrow cascading fountain caught the few shafts of sunlight that managed to pierce the gray San Francisco cloud cover.

A wealth of hidden beauty, difficult to discover, much like Nancy herself.

And now she was to be married!

I could picture Don, the groom, already beaming with joy. He was a short, chubby, kind fellow with wavy black hair and thick eyebrows. Don was employed as a mid-level manager in an insurance firm.

Secretly, I would have preferred someone more outgoing and yes, more successful for my daughter, but I fully realized that this was not my decision to make, and I had always kept my reservations to myself. I also knew that many boys had bypassed Nancy, in spite of her dark-haired, slender good looks, because of her reserved manner. Not every young man possessed the patience to wait for Nancy's wit and sharp intelligence to surface.

What I could not fathom were the evaluations of some of Nancy's more recent dates that had gotten back to me—comments that my alert, observant daughter, although polite and sweet, didn't really seem to "be there."

I didn't understand them at the time, but before this night was over, I would.

My husband David and son Ben, who was four years younger than 23-year-old Nancy, were already inside the Jewish Center to speak to the rabbi and to greet early-arriving guests. They had carried in Nancy's honeymoon luggage with them, but it remained for us to unload the cardboard boxes which contained the fragrant bridal bouquet, corsages, and boutonnieres from the car's trunk. Nancy reached out to take the some of the florist's parcels from me while she simultaneously attempted to shield me with her umbrella.

"No, it's okay, just be careful not to get your hair wet," I cautioned, "I hear the drowned-rat look is definitely out for brides!"

Laughing, Sonya, Nancy and I walked quickly, arms linked, as our heels clacked on the wet pavement. As we approached the glass doors of the temple's side entrance, I noticed a tall man walking inside, just a little ahead of us. Perhaps a Jewish Center official, I conjectured, as he went downstairs. Suddenly, I thought that I felt Nancy, who was holding my left arm, stiffen. I temporarily disregarded this fleeting perception as we stood under the temple's dark blue canopy and focused our attention on carefully shaking out our umbrellas before we entered. Only later did I realize my impression's significance.

"I think I'll go down to check my make-up," Nancy announced. "You go on ahead. I'll be up in a couple of minutes."

"We'll keep you company!" Sonya beamed. A "business" woman, she had never married, and treated Nancy like the daughter she had never had.

Perhaps it was my mother's intuition, but somehow I had the feeling that Nancy would have preferred to spend some time alone.

"Oh, come, Sonya, we have to greet everybody. Nancy will be up very soon."

Nancy smiled gratefully at me while I led a reluctant Sonya up several stairs and through the shiny, marble-floored hall to the rabbi's study.

Surprisingly, many guests had already arrived, although the hour was still early. Sonya spied tall Cousin Shirley, a secretary at Hunter College. Soon they were chatting animatedly. Some of the men joined with David and Don in a discussion with the young, bespectacled rabbi.

Good! Everyone seemed to be happily socializing, glad to meet at a *simcha* (happy occasion) and not at a funeral, but something nagged at me. Perhaps I *should* go down and check on Nancy. After I deposited my raingear and umbrella on the coat rack, I slipped out. Everyone seemed too engrossed in their conversations to notice my departure.

I walked quickly down the chilly hallway, past the office and the glass-enclosed cases where the colorful art projects of the Hebrew school students were exhibited.

As I descended the stairs, I passed a janitor who was going in the opposite direction. As he climbed up, his boom-box played a golden oldie song that I remembered from high school, "The Wayward Wind." I smiled, suddenly remembering the parody of this hit tune that my friends and I had created.

"The Kapusta*** Kid
Is a wayward kid,
A wild kid
Who's bound for cole slaw . . ."

My smile disappeared as my gaze took in the pail and mop that the janitor carried in his other hand, and the acrid smell of ammonia pinched my nostrils.

"How nice for the guests!" I thought sarcastically, shaking my head.

My disapproving focus shifted from the unsightly cleaning tools as voices drifted up to me, their volume increasing as the janitor and his radio moved further and further away.

Nancy was speaking to someone. I paused on the landing between the two staircases to push aside a strand of black hair that had escaped

*** A character created by the late comedian Ernie Kovacs. "Kapusta" means "cabbage" in several European languages.

my French-braid coiffure, and was annoyingly brushing against my eyelashes.

"How did you know that I was getting married tonight, Jack?" Nancy asked. Her voice drifted up to me. It was higher and thinner than usual.

Jack? Jack? Nancy had never mentioned someone named Jack. She had never dated anyone with that name that I knew of . . . unless . . . wait . . . There had been an administrator in Nancy's first school. With difficulty, his name came back to me—Jack Gordon!

If indeed this man was *that* Jack, he had been her mentor, and was about ten years older than Nancy. I recalled her remarking several times that he had been very helpful and how much she admired him, and then she had never mentioned him again. A year or so after she had begun her career in his school, she inexplicably transferred to a less desirable locale. She had refused to even discuss the change of venue.

The male voice replied to Nancy's question.

"I had to go into the Teachers' Room to ask Claire about a survey, and I heard Michelle talking about your wedding."

So it *was* Jack Gordon!

"She didn't see that you were at all interested, did she?" Nancy questioned anxiously. She was still in contact with some of her old friends who remained in Jack's school.

"No, of course not. I don't think she realized that I paid any attention whatsoever. Why should she?"

"Good." I heard Nancy give a tiny sigh of relief.

Jack continued in his satiny-smooth voice, "I've missed you so much!"

At this point, my hand tightened on the banister, its cold metal painfully chilling my fingers. Feathers of nausea tickled my throat, and my breath came in shallow gasps with the shock of the revelations that I was hearing.

"I've missed you, too."

"That's why I had to leave the school," Nancy continued, "the attraction was too strong. If I had stayed, I think something would have happened between us," my daughter confessed, her voice shaky.

"That wouldn't have been so terrible, Nancy."

"Of course it would have been! Look, Jack, you have a wife and four kids. I never had the stomach to be a home-wrecker, and I didn't want to wind up like Louisa Messina, alone and bitter, either."

I had met Louisa when I had gone to help Nancy decorate her first classroom the September that she began to teach. Louisa, petite and slender, had worn her dark hair pulled back in a chignon to show her classic features and olive skin. Over a period of fifteen years, she had faithfully waited for her physician boyfriend to leave his wife. Finally, the medical Don Juan had indeed filed for divorce—only to wed his young office technician.

"I would never do to you what that creep did to Louisa," Jack protested.

"Oh, I know that, but there was no way there could have been a good end to our situation. The only way we could ensure that nobody got hurt was not to be in contact, and to try and move ahead with our lives."

"So, Nancy, do you love this guy?" Jack asked, his voice quivering—wrinkles in the satin.

"Don was very patient. He knew that I was getting over someone. We get along well, we're really good friends with a lot of the same interests, and I feel he appreciates me and will always treat me well. Those are good things to base a marriage on. I love Don in a different way, and I'll try to be a good wife."

"Remember, I'll always love you."

"I'll always love you too, Jack." Each word that Nancy enunciated seemed to have a different pitch.

"Can I call you sometime?"

"No, I really don't think that would be a good idea. Listen, I've got to go." Nancy spoke so softly that I had trouble hearing her.

I realized that she was about to come upstairs. I couldn't let her know that I had been eavesdropping! I took a deep breath to compose myself.

"Nancy," I sang out loudly as I went down one step, my purple dress rustling with the movement, "Calling all brides!"

I could only hope that my levity would negate any suspicions Nancy might harbor that I had overheard her conversation with Jack.

"Coming, Mom," she replied in a strained voice. Almost immediately I spied her white-suited figure moving stiffly up the stairs, her raincoat folded neatly over her arm, her umbrella clenched in a white-knuckled hand. Her head was held high. Nancy's eyes were expressionless.

I turned, tottering slightly on my heels, hoping that the shakiness I felt was not apparent. Nancy began to follow me on what had suddenly become a long journey to the room where the wedding was to be held.

Once again, the janitor, minus his pail and mop, passed. This time, he carried only his radio. I could only hope that Nancy was too absorbed in reflecting on the emotions of the last few minutes to really comprehend the lyrics of the 60s song that was now playing. It was another old-time favorite that, with incredibly bad timing, was being featured at this very moment.

"Born too late for you to care,
Now my heart cries
Because your heart, it just couldn't wait.
Oh, why was I born too late?"

The ceremony was over quickly. Don crushed the symbolic glass with a soft, crunching sound—like life breaking hearts, I thought sadly.

There was a collective shout of "*Mazel tov!*"

Nancy and Don went ahead to the restaurant reception. They gave rides to Sonya, Cousin Shirley, and Don's single Uncle Irv.

David, Ben, and I walked through the drizzle to the Buick so that we could begin our own drive to the wedding dinner.

Around the edges of the car's windshield, where the wipers didn't quite reach, the Austin Street traffic light was shattered by the raindrops into glittering fragments of ruby, topaz, and emerald, like shards of broken dreams.

As we passed the Center's side entrance, I saw the tall man exiting slowly, his head bowed. My eyes burned, smearing my carefully applied make-up.

The car picked up speed. The rain spattered on the car's windows, not like drops of seltzer after all, but like the secret tears of a somber bride, taking bittersweet leave of her past, bravely facing towards her future.

SECRETS

"Bless the beasts and the children, for in this world they have no choice."
—*Rod McKuen*

1962

"You always have these secrets." My mother shook her dark head disapprovingly at me. She had taken a message from the Hunter College art department about an upcoming exhibit that was to include one of my paintings. The show was going to be held in a prestigious private Madison Avenue gallery.

"You never told us that the college chose your picture! Just like I had to find out that you were on the Dean's List when I made a mistake and opened the envelope that they sent you with the fancy announcement. And it's not like you have any friends who might have dropped the information."

She was clearly annoyed with both my reticence and my social isolation.

"It's no big deal," I shrugged. "I don't even like the picture that much myself, and I'm certainly not the only art student whose work they selected."

But, of course, my mother was right. I never talked about many things in my life—small awards I had received over my years in school, the invitation to a high school prom proffered by a pimply-faced boy (I was appalled—the thought of a male even touching my hand made my skin crawl), and the karate lessons that I took twice a week after college classes, so that I never again would be vulnerable. I hugged these small secrets to myself and used them as sort of insulating strips, wrapping them around the one big secret that could never be revealed.

BROOKLYN, 1948

"I'm looking over a four-leaf clover," I sang loudly as my favorite tune began to play. The song pulsed out of the jukebox—in my five-year-old mind a beautiful machine with rainbow borders of pink, green, and yellow that gave some measure of light to the dim neighborhood bar. Even more fascinating was the jukebox's metal arm that, with an almost human movement, reached out, selected a requested record, and slowly conveyed it to the turntable.

As soon as the music began to play, I ran quickly to Butch, the Airedale-mix who was the tavern's mascot, and placed his front paws on my shoulders. We managed to execute several dance steps as I supported him while he stood on his two hind legs.

"Yay, Joanie, yay, Butch," cheered the laughing patrons, including my father, who always brought me along when he stopped by for his usual Sunday beer. His tanned hand raised a golden liquid-filled glass high in a mock toast.

When Butch tired, we ran to the built-in bench that was covered in faux red leather and lay head to head, inhaling the oddly salty odor of the upholstery. We must have been quite a sight—me in my green checked Sunday dress and white hair bow, and the beige dog with his big brown eyes.

After a few minutes, we recovered enough to be coaxed back to continue our show. When we finally completed our act a couple of songs later, we were roundly applauded, and our enthusiastic audience, amused and good-humored because of our performance, ordered more drinks. We were good for business!

Charlie the bartender handed me a brown dog biscuit to be fed to Butch, and presented me with a sparkling coke that was topped by a bright maraschino cherry. I always held the cola up to one of the room's dim lights to see the garnet flash in the dark liquid. Then I delightedly drank it down, relishing the beverage's cold, sweet taste in my hot, dry mouth and giggling as the bubbles gently tickled my nose.

As soon as I finished the soda, it was time to see my friend Alice. I ran through the back room, where extra liquor, dishtowels, and clean glasses were stored, and into the yard that the bar shared with a large gray apartment house.

Alice was a tall, thin girl with blond curly hair that seemed unable to be wholly contained by the white barrettes she always wore. Alice was four years older than I was, but never patronized me or bossed me around. She was unfailingly patient and treated me with good humor.

"I always wanted a little sister," she confided, gently patting my shoulder. Her friendship actualized my own dreams of having a big sister, so our childhood aspirations meshed well and brought us much of the joy of childhood. At least for a time.

One day Alice motioned me to join her in the apartment house's basement.

"Oh, no," I replied quickly. "My mother said never to go into a cellar."

"Well, of course not, silly. But you're with me, and I'm much older. And, don't forget," she added proudly, lifting her chin slightly and smiling down at me, "My father's the super!"

I couldn't forget. One day Alice had introduced me to a tall, slim man in blue overalls. He had straight blond hair and a short, turned-up nose. His voice was loud and raspy, like the "voice" of a diesel train on the record that my kindergarten teacher had played.

I found it odd that everyone, even Alice, called him "Ned." Despite her informality, I sensed that she somehow feared him.

When he met me, Ned regarded me for a few seconds and then said, "Yeah, girlie," a strange response, even to the ears of a five-year-old.

He turned to leave, but then suddenly whirled around to face us again. With his finger on his chin, he asked with a sneer, "Hey, ain't you the kid who dances with the dog?" Before I could even reply, he quickly turned once more and left.

I wasn't sorry that he had departed. Ned seemed to be a negative and nasty person. Even his name sounded like "*nyet*," the word my mother had told me meant "no" in Russian.

Alice led me down three steps, opened the brown wooden door, and pulled a string to switch on the naked light bulb. Cool, musty air rose up from the gray cement floor, but despite the drab walls, the cellar was a child's dream play area. There were brown wooden barrels to hide behind, beige cardboard boxes containing hidden treasure (actually goods stored by tenants), and even an old mahogany piano for us to bang on.

We happily pushed a rickety baby carriage that was not currently in use by its owner. I joyously rode a rusty tricycle over the uneven floor.

The bumps added excitement to my trip around the few areas of the basement that remained uncluttered. In another room, the coal bin held gleaming ebony riches, but Alice warned against going anywhere in its vicinity. Close contact would make us *very* dirty, she cautioned, and wrinkled her nose in disgust.

Nevertheless, there were enough other diversions to create an imaginative child's paradise. This cellar was a wonderful place! My mother's warning had never seemed so irrelevant.

An almost daily routine began. During the week, my mother would bring me up to the bar's entrance—in the 1940s, no decent woman would dream of entering such an establishment unescorted. Then she would sit with a book on one of the benches that lined Parkside Avenue and read as she waited for me while I played with Alice. Of course, Mother thought that we were just having fun in the bar's backyard, and had no idea that we were enjoying subterranean amusements.

My friendship with Alice came at a particularly opportune time; just when the neighborhood children had summer vacation, the Prospect Park playground where we all met was closed for renovations. I missed the swings and slides; I missed having a place to see my friends and win their attention and approval as I joined them in games and led them in songs.

At first, it seemed to be just another humid, cloudy summer day in Brooklyn. The slight breeze that filtered through the brown screen door of our apartment failed to bring any relief—just more humidity-laden heavy air. Any movement caused beads of perspiration to form on my face, and even the whirring black fan provided little respite. My usual perky bow couldn't disguise the fact that my hair hung in damp brown strings.

Nevertheless, my mother and I set out for my play-date with Alice. I fervently hoped that my friend was waiting; she had not shown up twice in the last week, and I had dejectedly left the bar, head lowered in disappointment. Even a vanilla and chocolate Dixie cup with a movie star's picture inside the lid had failed to cheer me.

As usual, after leaving my mother, I ran through the bar, barely noticing the pre-noon drinkers, nor the crystalline bottles of amber liquid that were reflected in the mirrors behind the shelves. I stopped briefly to greet Charlie, and to give a quick hug to Butch, whose tongue lolled out of his mouth, and who lay directly under the ceiling fan in a vain attempt to cool himself.

Alice was not in the yard. It was too muggy to wait outside, so I carefully opened the door to the basement and entered. Perhaps, I thought, my friend was inside where it was, at least, slightly cooler. I pulled the string to turn on the light and peered around. Maybe Alice, who loved jokes, was hiding in back of some of the boxes, or perhaps she was standing behind one of the gray arches that subdivided the cellar's areas. I took a few steps forward and tentatively called, "Alice, Alice!" There was only silence that was as solid as the concrete walls.

Suddenly I felt my arms being pinned hard against my body as I was grabbed from behind and lifted off the ground. I knew, even before I turned my head, who my assailant was.

"What do you want, girlie?" Ned demanded, still holding me high off the floor. He moved his face closer to mine. He reeked of alcohol.

"Oh, I was just looking for Alice. Is she coming?" I managed to stammer. I attempted to smile.

"Nah, Alice ain't here today," Ned replied. With a nasty laugh, he said, "C'mere, girlie!"

With that, he pushed me down on the cold cement floor, and I felt an enormous pressure crushing me so hard that I couldn't breathe.

I must have blacked out, because the next things I remembered were freedom from the enormous weight that had taken my breath away, and the glint of metal from a knife similar to the one my father took along when he went fishing.

I felt a scratch on my upper right thigh that immediately began to sting and then morphed into an increasingly searing pain. It coalesced with the smarting inside me to create an ever-increasing conflagration throughout my lower body. My leg felt wet, and I knew, even before I looked, that I was bleeding from a cut that was not very deep, but that ran several inches on my pale skin. The burning agony rose to my eyes, but although they were tearing, I was too frightened and too frozen to really cry. I could only moan softly.

"Now when your mama sees your drawers, she won't ask any stupid questions about how you got so bloody there." Ned gave a long, chortling laugh as he zipped up the front of his overalls. Then he pulled me roughly to my feet. He bent down and looked directly into my eyes.

"You ever tell, I'll kill that dog of yours, and then I'll come and kill your family, too. Got that?"

His voice was raspier than ever, and the stench of bitter beer was sickening, but I dared not avert my face.

"Yes," I barely managed to whisper.

"Good. Remember what I said. Now go back to your mama; she's waiting."

He lifted the hem of my dress, smirked, and gave me a shove in the direction of the door.

"Hurry up, girlie, she's waiting," he repeated. *"Hurry up, damn ya!"*

I scurried out through the bar, without even looking at Butch or saying my usual good-byes to Charlie.

My mother *was* impatiently waiting for me. She was already standing up next to the bench and smoothing her flowered dress with quick, heavy strokes.

"It's about time you came back. It looks like it's going to come down any minute. Did you have fun? Oh, and look at you; you're bleeding. Does it hurt? We'll clean you up as soon as we get home. What did you do, fall?"

Her comments and questions fell on the thick air faster than the anticipated showers that would soon saturate the neighborhood.

"Yeah, I mumbled, and with uncharacteristic restraint, walked close to my mother, not skipping or singing as I usually did. Mother probably attributed my lack of enthusiasm to the heat and humidity, as well as to my injury. We hurried along, trying to beat the imminent rain.

How could she know that my body felt sore and far dirtier than my entire bottle of green bubble bath could ever cleanse and purify?

For the duration of the next several days, I alternated between sleeping and, as I listlessly lay on my cot, staring out the window at the cityscape of rooftops and the sliver of Flatbush Avenue that was visible below. There was good reason for my daytime lethargy. I was remaining awake for much of each night, afraid of experiencing the recurring nightmares that haunted my sleep, and anxious that my restlessness would disturb my parents, whose room I shared.

They had already begun to regard me with worried expressions, especially when I feigned stomach pains to avoid going anywhere outside our small apartment. I believed that the security of our four walls was the only thing that protected me from the thing that I feared the most—another encounter with Ned.

Finally, the pediatrician was called to visit me at home. Dr. Hamill examined me, but besides some weight loss because of my lack of appetite, he could find nothing really wrong. Years later, I wondered how the doctor could so cavalierly dismiss symptoms that, even in that more naïve time, should have been a cause for concern.

"Oh, don't worry, Mrs. Gerstein," the doctor grinned. "Joanie's just going through a stage. In a week or two she'll be back to her usual chatterbox self."

My mother, relieved, returned his smile. In the 1940s, a physician's word was almost a holy pronouncement.

Several days after the pediatrician's fruitless house call, I was still spending most of the time in bed. Heat and humidity continued to hang over the city, smothering its energy and vitality in the same way that Ned's weight had crushed the breath out of me. The late-day air that slowly seeped into the house brought no cooling relief, just more sultry discomfort.

Suddenly I heard the screen door open, then close—the signal that my father had returned from work. His voice had an unusual sense of urgency as he greeted my mother in the narrow hallway. Leaning on my right forearm, I sat partly up to hear their conversation.

"Subway . . . slow . . . hot. Went . . . bar . . . cool off . . . beer," my father's words floated faintly through the apartment. "Butch the dog . . . poisoned."

I fell back on my pillow as if shoved by an unseen hand. Stunned, I drew my knees to my chest in a fetal position of grief and shock.

Immediately I realized that Ned had to be responsible. Butch was confined to the yard and to the bar, and he was only allowed on the street when he was walked on a leash by Charlie. If Ned had meant to send me the message that he could follow through on his threats, he had certainly succeeded. Remembering his evil warnings, I trembled for my parents' safety. Would they be next?

As if to confirm my suspicions, my father continued, "Charlie found . . . bad meat . . . yard. Who could . . . ? We'll tell . . . went to . . . farm . . . New Hampshire," he concluded.

"Sure, have to tell . . . something," my mother replied. Then, with a loud groan, she added, " . . . all she needs . . . dog won't be . . ."

My father walked slowly into the bedroom. He was still wearing his yellow straw summer hat. When he told me that Butch had gone to live in New Hampshire, I nodded solemnly. Now, more than ever, I believed that the only hope for my family's survival was in the most stringent guarding of "the secret." I would have to be the best actress!

I strove to behave with some semblance of normalcy. While at no time did either parent suggest a return visit to the bar—they probably assumed that I would be too sad not to see my "dancing partner"—I did go to the newly renovated park playground. I also managed to choke down some of my formerly favorite foods.

Despite my best efforts, I was a shell of the carefree, happy child that I had been just a few weeks before.

About a month later, in the beginning of August, my mother gave me a big smile and in a louder than usual voice announced, "Guess what? We're moving to Queens! You'll have your own room! You're going to start first grade in a new school! Isn't that wonderful?"

The projected move was not a total shock; my parents had discussed getting a larger apartment for years. Now my Aunt Pearl had found one for us, right in her Forest Hills neighborhood.

Before the horrific events in the cellar, I would have been devastated if the relocation had actually materialized. I had loved my Brooklyn life—Butch, the bar, my friends, and the oasis of nature's beauty that was Prospect Park. Now I felt a small measure of relief—we would be far from Ned, and therefore *somewhat* safer. But it would be years before I could walk down the street, even in Queens, without looking over my shoulder, half-expecting to see Ned behind me, poised to perpetrate evil.

Queens, 1948

The new apartment building was situated high on a hill. It was surrounded by one-family residences, including Aunt Pearl's attached home. Cool breezes swirled through our rooms, in which newly painted white walls gleamed, filling the air with a sweetish odor.

At first, I was invited to the parties of neighbor children and new classmates. The bright blue, red, and yellow balloons seemed to almost vibrate with excitement. The birthday cake, with its pastel pink and green icing, held the promise of sweet, soft bliss.

But then a gray concrete veil would fall over the festive scene, leaching it of color and light. I would sit huddled in a corner, watching the other children celebrating as they screamed, laughed, and ran. They were having the fun that I deemed myself too guilty—for disobeying my mother's injunction and indirectly causing Butch's death—and too soiled to deserve.

Soon enough, the invitations stopped. Probably, no one wanted such a little sad-sack putting a damper on their parties. My mother was understandably upset, but I was secretly relieved. It was too painful to watch everybody else enjoying the good things that I felt unworthy of.

My parents, still concerned, continued to quiz me, asking "What's wrong?" and "Are you okay?" as they peered at me, their brows furrowed with concern.

Eventually, I was taken to a new doctor, a Queens doctor. Because he had never known the old, extroverted Joanie, he could not properly evaluate the 180-degree personality change that had occurred. There seemed to be no physical issues that needed to be addressed, he stated, shaking his head. He murmured something about over-protective parents of only children, and dismissed us with a wave of his hand.

My parents, somewhat reassured, lessened their scrutiny.

They were also encouraged by my progress in school, where I soon led my class in reading, math, and art. My mother and father did not know that it was only while I was concentrating on decoding words, solving problems with numbers, and crayoning or painting that I could, at least for a time, ignore the gnawing pain in my chest, and have a brief respite from flashbacks of gray concrete cellars and raspy-voiced predators.

My art work reflected my turbulent emotions—dull, drab colors on the periphery, and bold, angry hues in the center.

November, 1961

It was because of the preparations for the art exhibit I had neglected to inform my mother about that I found myself in the Lexington Avenue and Fifty-Ninth Street subway station far later than usual. I would just be able to catch the evening's last Queens-bound RR train at 7:30.

The interminable discussions and paperwork for the gallery show were encroaching on the hours that I worked as a student aide in the

Hunter College library. This art "honor" was becoming expensive! Adding to my annoyance was the large oak tag cylinder that I had to lug home—a returned piece of work from a different project. I began to walk to the front of the station. My irritation must have shown in the hard, quick steps that I took on the gray concrete.

I noted that there were far too many passengers waiting on the other side of the platform, where the Brooklyn-bound trains ran, than normal for this post rush-hour time. There must be some delays, I grimly conjectured. Such crowds were not a good sign! During my years of traveling in the New York City subway system, I had observed that even the smallest slowdown in one direction often precipitated lateness on the opposite route, like a sympathetic physiological reaction in which one eye is injured, but the other one tears. I certainly hoped that this would not be the case tonight. I was really tired!

"*@#* train," someone rasped out. "*Hurry up, damn ya!*"

The voice was the voice of my nightmares, but I wasn't at home in my bed. Quickly, fearfully, my eyes swept the crowd. Sure enough, towering over the commuters, Ned stood scowling.

He hadn't changed much in thirteen years. His blond hair was a little thinner and grayer, and he had developed a bit of a beer belly, which protruded from the open khaki jacket that seemed too thin for the chill autumn evening, but I would have known him anywhere.

An icy wave began at the top of my head and swept down my body to my feet. A sharp pain twisted my stomach, and the station's lights seemed to be rapidly growing dimmer. Breathing became difficult, and I knew that I was just seconds from passing out.

That could not happen! I took several slow, deep breaths as I stood suddenly still while others pushed their way past me. Gradually, the lights became brighter once again.

It wasn't too difficult for me to get close to Ned, for although the platform was crowded, people were attempting to step away from the loudly cursing, erratically shifting commuter who, I realized as I came closer, reeked of alcohol.

Ned once again turned his attention to the tunnel, from which the tardy train had yet to emerge. And now, I was thankful for the hours of karate practice that I had pushed my exhausted body through. I was also suddenly grateful for the oak tag that I held cross-wise in front of me. The large roll served to block the view of my knife-scarred right leg pushing hard against the back of Ned's knees. My strong right hand, powered by years of suppressed rage, was catapulted out of the "chamber" (position in which the fist is held close to the body) and executed a 180-degree twist that landed in the small of his back.

In the distance, a train's imminent approach was signaled with ever-increasing static that was rapidly morphing into a roar. Just a split second before my blows landed, Ned had extended his upper body over the platform's edge and yelled one last time, "*Hurry up, damn ya!*"

It was the last thing he ever said. The angle that he had assumed made my strikes even more effective, and Ned was easily catapulted on to the track, just ahead of the oncoming train. I could hear the hiss of the third rail as it burned the flesh off his head and neck. The crowd gave a gasp of horror as sparks flew nearly platform-high. The acrid smell of smoke stung my nose, the way uncried tears had, for so long, stung my eyes. Ned disappeared under the first car.

I turned, lowering my head and putting my free hand to my mouth, as if in shock. Despite the density of the crowd, people quickly made way for me to come through, probably less out of concern for my well-being than because of a desire not to be fainted or vomited upon.

I returned quickly to the back of the station as Transit Authority police ran in the opposite direction, rushing to the accident scene. As they hurried, their batons swung rhythmically against their sides. A slight breeze blew out of the tunnel and over my teeth. I realized that for the first time in thirteen years, I was really smiling because some measure of justice had finally been attained, and I had given myself a small sense of closure.

I wondered how many little girls had been saved from lives of misery, degradation, and even suicide by my actions of that evening.

The image of Butch's soulful eyes suddenly flashed through my mind. The poor dog's only sin was that he had been my gentle playmate, and he had died because of it. Now he, too, had been avenged.

The newspapers on the following day were filled with gruesome accounts of Ned's demise. They described how, even though the train's engineer had heroically tried to apply the brakes, three cars had passed over the victim, slicing him, in the words of an EMT, "into bloody ribbons."

Witnesses had recalled the deceased's bizarre behavior and the overwhelming smell of the alcohol that he had obviously indulged in.

Ned's death was deemed a horrific accident, caused by the victim's failure to adhere to common-sense safety practices. I carefully checked all of the television, radio, and newspaper reports of the "accident" with the diligence of a veteran detective. Would Alice be named as a surviving relative?

My painstaking efforts were unrewarded. There were no references to any family members. However, an account in the *New York Post* mentioned that final arrangements for the unfortunate victim were being handled by the Norris Funeral Home in Brooklyn.

I decided that I would place the call from Hunter to avoid my mother overhearing my conversation. It would also be impossible, I reasoned, to trace it in the very unlikely event that someone became curious as to the identity of the person who had phoned. The college had thousands of students.

I took the elevator to the cafeteria level in the time between my sociology and art classes. There, an array of telephone directories from Manhattan, Queens, Brooklyn, the Bronx, and Staten Island attested to the diverse home boroughs of Hunter's population.

I quickly turned the tissue-thin, worn Brooklyn White Pages to the N's. The Norris Funeral Home was conveniently located in Cypress Hills near several cemeteries, the sidebar ad indicated in bold type.

With trembling fingers I inserted a dime into the phone's silver coin slot and dialed the number. Would I finally find Alice?

At first, I thought I had reached a woman representative of the establishment. As the conversation progressed, I realized that I was speaking to a man with a high-pitched voice.

"Norris Funeral Home. Your memories are our sacred trust. How can we help you?"

"I wanted to know; is there a wake for the man who was killed in the subway? His daughter Alice was my friend when we were children."

"And you called after all this time? How nice of you. Death does bring people together!"

The voice was cloyingly sweet, probably an automatic response after years of comforting mourners. I wrinkled my nose in distaste.

"Let me check for you." The receiver was put down with a gentle tap. About thirty seconds later I heard an intake of breath, followed by the rustle of paper.

"No, there will be no wake. A cremation service will be held tomorrow, but I'm so sorry to tell you, there's nothing here about your friend, the daughter. Only the brother, Mr. Charles Ferguson, is listed as a family member."

"No one else?" I inquired, my voice trembling.

"No." The paper rustled again as it was re-checked. "I'm sorry."

"Thank you for your time," I managed to stammer.

"I regret that we couldn't be of more help. And please remember, in times of loss, the Norris Funeral Home stands ready to serve."

Shakily, I replaced the phone. Had Alice severed ties with her monster father, or had harm come to her at his hands?

Sadly, I was never to learn the fate of my beloved friend.

Epilogue

A few terms later, I graduated Hunter with high honors. I found a job with the New York City library system. I was assigned to lead the story hour, during which I would read and discuss literature with elementary school pupils.

I began to specialize in books that dealt with issues of child safety, in such tomes as *Strangers Are Not Always Friends* and *Jennifer and Jason's Neighborhood Walk*.

My efforts have earned me a folder bulging with letters of commendation and gratitude from parents, teachers, and police precincts.

I adopted an Airedale mix from Animal Control and named him Butch. He had been abused and abandoned, but under my care he became a faithful and loving companion, and my only friend.

Sometimes when I look at him and pat his soft beige fur, I think back to a long ago time when a dog very much like him danced with a little Brooklyn girl who wore green checks—two innocents blissfully unaware of the impending evil that would slither out of the shadows to destroy both of their lives.

Ruby

Glowing crimson facets
Bright and dark gradations,
If I stare long enough
Hypnotized by carmine gleam,
Soft red light enveloping me,
Cherry Jell-O depths revealing
A corridor to past years,
A gateway to my memories,
Of glowing, joyous bygone times,
So that I can live, once again, in
The scarlet brilliance of youth.

FRAGMENTS
OF
FAREWELL

Part of the process of coming to terms with our mortality is saying a final good-bye to places that have been very pivotal parts of our lives by giving us moments of joy and beauty.

Our farewells are as the wrapping and ribbons on a gift box—a tribute to the best experiences of our days, an opportunity for appreciation and sad but thankful closure.

LIFE JOURNEY

"In the morning, I check the obituaries, and if my name isn't listed, I have a good day!" So goes the old joke.

Indeed, my daily perusal of the death notices is a subject of merriment amongst my friends. However, reading the obits is really a serious business. By checking them, I have gleaned information about people from my past, including playmates from childhood whose parents had passed on. I have even been reunited with a high school friend when I called to express condolences.

Sadly, a few times my peers themselves were listed as deceased. I had always managed to distance myself from their deaths—"they were older"—a year or two—or "accidents can happen to anyone"—until the day that I read, with sorrow and dismay, of the death of Mike Garber.

"Oh no," I exclaimed in horror, as I tremblingly dropped the long black and white sheet on the kitchen table, next to my rapidly cooling coffee.

Mike had moved into the canyons of Forest Hills apartment buildings in our junior year of high school. He had been tall and handsome with brown hair, green eyes, and a husky muscular build that bespoke athletic prowess. Mike's arrival was immediately noted by the school's more sophisticated and well-groomed young ladies. Therefore, it was something of a shock when he was sent as a monitor to the bookroom where I worked, and after a short period of joking banter, he asked me for a date. To the young, naïve girl that I was, such a coup was nothing short of miraculous.

For a short while, I was able to relish the envy of other girls, as I walked just a little bit taller, and applied just a little bit more make-up.

In time, Mike moved on, leaving me slumped and broken-hearted, but in my mind he had always symbolized youthful vitality, high spirits, and future promise.

Now he was dead, and all of my rationalizations were gone as well, like the bloom of sixties prom corsages. Mortality loomed.

It was time to re-examine my life. But how?

Visions of blue-tiled mosques in Samarkand, the cobalt waters of Lake Baikal, and Indian workers clinging desperately to commuter trains like the shipwrecked to driftwood ran through my memory. These sights from the TV series "Great Railway Journeys" contrasted sharply with the dirty ocher tiles and gray-brown concrete of my local subway station.

On this fall morning, I was traveling from Forest Hills, where I still lived, to Manhattan to shop and, hopefully, to dissipate some of the depression that I had felt in the past weeks since learning about Mike's passing.

My neighborhood had become quite ethnically diverse over the years, but background differences seemed less conspicuous because of the similar, almost uniform type of casual clothing worn by so many riders.

The only distinctive, interesting passenger was an Asian woman in a beige pants suit who was pushing a green suitcase-on-wheels. Periodically, she slapped her left shoulder with her left hand. I was wondering if she was performing a t'ai chi-type exercise, or if she was just another New York nut, when the train noisily arrived.

As I took my seat in the beige and orange subway car, I had a revelation—a flash so bright and sharp that my eyes actually blinked.

To hell with purchasing clothing that I didn't really need! I would take my very own great train journey to the past days of my life.

The train gently rocked and softly clicked—perhaps a sign of approval?

We pulled into the Lexington Avenue stop. I could visualize myself as a pony-tailed teenager flushed with the excitement of the college experience as I ran up the stairs to the "6" train that would continue to convey me to Hunter.

Only a few years later, I would slowly trudge up those same steps, stooped with exhaustion after a day of teaching, to attend graduate school.

At the dimly lit Forty-Second Street station, I remembered when my fiancé, later my husband, worked in this area. We would meet for lunch or dinner dates at his office. On the ride in, I would frequently check my appearance in the train's dirty window glass.

One of the lower Manhattan stations on today's route was the transfer point to East New York, the Brooklyn neighborhood where I had taught for almost thirty years. In that part of the city, the sooty elevated trains were silhouetted against the bleak gray sky as they crawled between the dilapidated apartment houses and the shabby private dwellings.

Close by, the salmon-hued, Victorian-style school loomed over the poorly maintained, trash-strewn building rooftops. I could envision ghosts of departed colleagues hovering about P.S. 108's gabled turrets and I could almost hear the shrill voices of children in the tiny, crowded yard.

We continued to Court Street, the first Brooklyn stop on this subway line. The Board of Education's offices had been located here. I remembered when all of us hopeful and eager new graduates trembled with anxiety, and prayed that the myriad necessary bureaucratic forms were in order so that we could begin our teaching careers. How our idealism contrasted with the attitudes of the mostly rude and lazy clerks of all races and creeds, united in the brotherhood of politically appointed privilege and incompetent sloth.

Further along the curving subway tracks lay the neighborhood of my earliest years—Flatbush. More than fifty years before, I had proudly started kindergarten here. I recalled the teacher showing us the red coffee beans that so wondrously echoed the hue of the autumnal leaves as they glowed in the afternoon sunshine.

In the late forties, our friend Irving sold flowers in the Parkside Avenue Station. I could still remember the heavy moist air, thick with the blossoms' fragrance. He always insisted on pressing sweet-smelling carnations into my small hand and never accepted payment for these gifts. ("Try not to take," Mother cautioned. "He's a poor man.")

He was surely long gone from there, but to the left of the covered station that was neither underground nor elevated, the treetops of Prospect Park still towered majestically. As I raised my head to pay them proper tribute, images of that beautiful oasis came to me, and all of the childhood adventures that had played out there were resurrected in my mind. I could almost feel the gritty, icy wetness that penetrated my clothes and boots as the sled that my father and I had ridden turned over, and I felt laughter rising up as it had on that winter day so long ago.

Not far from the station lay Flatbush Avenue, with its remembered delightful sights and smells. In shop windows, cold sweet Charlotte Russes, their creamy white crowns embellished with ruby cherries, had tempted passers-by. At the beginning of February, the bittersweet aromas that pervaded Barton's Chocolate Shop had already been captured in crimson foil heart-shaped boxes that, to a child's eye, were not mere containers, but objects of indescribable beauty.

At this point, I was sorely tempted to leave the train and attempt to rediscover the landmarks that were etched in my mind. Good sense, though, overrode my impulse. I had already heard that the Patio Movie Theater and adjoining ice cream parlor had been leveled for a housing project. What other unspeakable mutilations of beloved memories awaited? Then too, there were other, practical consideration. The quiet and friendly tree-shaded streets of bygone days were now the backdrop for sporadic crime waves and shootings. I preferred that my great train journey would not also be my final excursion!

With an unusually loud burst of noise and a very strong forward motion, the train emerged from the station into glaring daylight that caused my eyes to burn. Or were those tears?

I rode until Coney Island, the end of the line, and then crossed over to the opposite side to catch a return train. From a window on the staircase, I caught sight of the now-deserted beach whose beige-silver sand stretched languidly to the dark turquoise ocean.

Suddenly, it was not October but July, and I was again the small child running after my father's army uniform, only to weep bitterly on finding that the wearer was, after all, a stranger. My terrified aunt had gasped with exhaustion and panic as she finally managed to catch up to me on the jammed, hot beach.

I was now heading back to Manhattan. I decided to visit an art exhibit that was being held on Fifty-Seventh Street. Once there, I quickly exited the train and climbed to the mezzanine. Just as quickly though, I realized that even the most beautiful show would break the mood of this day. What I needed was to go home. I just wasn't sure, for several seconds, in which direction to travel.

A SHOWER OF MEMORIES

I will never return to that place.

As I drove down Linwood Street, I vividly remembered every driveway, every hydrant, and every tree, just as on the ride over my hands on the steering wheel had anticipated every one of the Interboro Parkway's myriad curves and slopes.

And why not? I had made this trip daily, for almost thirty years, to teach at Brooklyn's P.S. 108.

A little farther down Linwood, after the light on Ridgewood Avenue, I could see the orange armory-like façade of the school towering over the neighborhood's shabby gray one—and two—family homes. The gabled building had not substantially changed over the forty years since I had first beheld it, when I had been a newly appointed teacher. It had been a sunny, crisp early fall morning, not unlike today. Even now, I still smiled at my humorous first impression that an architect had gone wild with hundreds of tons of canned salmon and constructed a school.

I lifted my eyes to the windows of the third-floor room that had been my domain for so long. I had observed seasonal changes through the glass during those years—the chartreuse of spring and summer gardens, the red and yellow autumn leaves, and overwhelmingly, the gray streets of winter. On clear days, above the treetops of Highland Park, I could see the Interboro snaking against the sky. In the darkness of Open School Nights, the parkway lights seemed to form a new constellation radiating from the ebony heavens.

Although I had retired some years before, I was visiting to attend a wedding shower for one of my few remaining former colleagues. It wasn't as though I had cut all ties to the school; I continued to socialize with many of the people whom I had met at P.S. 108. Now, they too were retired. However, since I had left teaching, I had never had the occasion to return to the building itself until today.

I parked the car and carefully carried my large purple and white gift box down Linwood Street.

A screeching "J" train thundered by just then, speeding along the elevated tracks one block away, down on Fulton Street. The gray cars were almost toy-like as they quickly flashed by in the sunlight, as fleeting as my own youthful dreams.

The school's first floor was exactly as it appeared in the archives of my memory. There was still the same green-and-black linoleum, still the same drab pale pink walls.

My perception of being in a time warp was unceremoniously shattered by the female security guard's request that I sign the brown visitors' book. I was now officially a stranger in the place that had been my second home for so long. The school had been the backdrop for a myriad of pivotal life events—crisp beginnings, family illnesses and deaths, marriage, career decisions and many friendships. It was as if I had sampled a bittersweet candy and it had touched a tooth with a newly revealed exposed nerve.

I climbed the grille-enclosed staircase to the second floor. A few veteran teachers greeted me with hugs and words of welcome, but the majority of the staff passed by and regarded me with curious looks. How could they recognize me? It had been, after all, eleven years since I had been a part of what had once been a very close-knit faculty, almost a semi-family.

The Teachers' Room was decorated beautifully and looked more splendid than I had ever imagined it could appear. Pink, yellow, and white tissue flowers were strewn everywhere. Red construction paper placemats covered the nondescript beige Formica tables. By dint of white crepe paper and artistic sleight of hand, an ordinary tan metal schoolroom chair had been transformed into a throne for the bride-to-be that was worthy of such a "celebrity" educator.

Foil warming pans, still covered, held the promise of sumptuous delicacies, a future hope bolstered by the spicy, sweet and pungent aromas that were already beginning to rise into the warm air.

But the plaque was nowhere to be seen.

A wooden and bronze plaque had been created to memorialize Maxine Wertheim, a dedicated, kind, and popular teacher whose terrific sense of humor used to lighten our grayest days, and had encouraged us in our most frustrating moments. She had passed away at a young age, leaving a gaping hole in the faculty and sadness in the hearts of so many.

I looked around at the now-arriving current staff, who seemed to be almost childishly youthful. Most had never known Maxine, who had died almost twenty years before, when the majority of these new teachers had been small children. Now that the plaque was no longer hanging in the room, it seemed as though, at least in terms of the school, Maxine had never existed.

The red-haired, vivacious guest of honor cried tears of joy as she opened and displayed each gift. Cheers followed each exhibition. Happy party noise nearly drowned out high-pitched expressions of gratitude. Flashbulbs popped, glaringly recording the celebration. The newly installed air conditioner was unequal to cooling the overcrowded room, and faces grew shiny and moist even as more hot food was ingested.

As soon as the presents were unwrapped and good wishes extended, I took my leave.

A famous rabbi once said that often when we do something for the very last time—play a childhood game, visit a beloved place—we don't even realize that this time is, indeed, the last. However, as I walked briskly up Linwood Street I was quite sure that I would never return to 108. Today's glimpse of the forty years that had vanished so quickly, so quickly, the passing of my life—was enough of a foretaste of my own mortality to warrant a self-imposed exile.

A Transformed Perspective

Sharply turning away from the roller coaster
With a terrified shake of the head
The ride that once rocketed me past my limits,
And made me soar with the wind on my teeth.
The rush of speed-induced pressure between my eyes,
And the illusion of invincibility
As fleeting as the wild journey's duration.

I close my ears to the music whose notes, in days past,
Sent my spirit soaring towards the sun
As my heart beat passionately with thoughts of love,
And laughter rose in my now silent throat.

I take no deep breaths in the brightly lit bakery
That overflows with aromatic confections,
Now indifferent to the heavy, warm air
That's suffused with sugary vanilla fragrance,
The strong, bittersweet perfume of chocolate,
And promises of calorie-induced bliss.
The focus is only on the purchase of sour rye.

Bright, foil—wrapped presents disinterestedly set aside,
Joyous anticipation long forgotten,
As shiny ribbons remain tied, lovingly crafted
Into coils of blue and pink, crowning unopened gifts.

When did life's vibrant rainbow fade to dull gray
And my spirit's effervescence evaporate
Like seltzer bubbles into warm air?
When did I grow old?

A Last Resort

"He couldn't be playing *that* song!" I thought with surprise as I shook my head incredulously.

My husband and I had just returned, after an absence of over three years, to the Catskill resort that had been our vacation venue for many summers.

We were not the only long-time guests whose visits had slowed, whose focus had shifted. More opulent, newer locales that featured gambling and easier access had diverted vacationers with their siren songs and slick ads. Because of the area's gradual decline after halcyon days that had extended into the 1980s, most resorts in this region had already shuttered. Once-glorious pleasure domes that had vibrated with pulsating, almost garish life were now empty hulks, forlorn ships abandoned in seas of lush countryside vegetation and waves of rolling green hills. All that remained of them were sequined memories, lightly floating on the clear Catskill air.

But now rumors that this hotel had been sold, that it too would soon be closed, had come to the fore, like bubbles breaking the surface tension of a glass of seltzer. We had come this summer to bid a possible farewell to our bucolic home away from home.

And now Joe, the elderly gentleman who specialized in entertaining guests with "golden oldies", was harmonizing with his accordion to "My Prayer."

There must be some mistake. That song's from my teenage years, and not a golden oldie at all. What was Joe thinking, I wondered.

"That you'll always be there!" Joe concluded triumphantly, his voice cracking slightly as he hit the song's highest notes.

Now maybe he would play one of the vintage tunes that he had always been noted for . . . perhaps "Make Believe," a song that had been my mother's favorite.

Instead, "Whenever I want you, all I have to do is dream, dream, dream, all I have to do is dream!" rang out.

But that Everly Brothers classic had been popular in my adolescence. What was going on? Why, a golden oldie had to have been current at least fifty years ago . . .

And then, like the violent jerk from the sudden braking of a car, the realization hit me. It *was* fifty years!

The revelation was so unsettling, so shattering, that I had to sit down on one of the lobby's overstuffed, pale green sofas.

Without having been quite in the moment, without consciously experiencing the journey, I had drifted over the line into senior citizenship. My once au-courant frames of reference now sported an antique patina.

And it was not just I who had aged, I realized sadly as I looked around the lobby, where the green and pink flowered carpeting was noticeably faded. The once-elegant upholstered furniture had a shabby, worn look, and sagged with the burden of seating guests for so many years.

Absent was the clean, antiseptic smell of Lysol, a product once proudly endorsed by the hotel. Instead, a delicate hint of the mustiness (perhaps caused by the proximity of a small lake) that also pervaded many of the guest rooms wafted through the resort. The slight but unpleasant odor symbolized its deterioration and careless administration, possibly born of the resignation and depression that currently existed in the hostelry.

Checking in at the long brown mahogany counter, bright with fluorescent lighting, had seemed more flawed now, with slow-moving, uncertain clerks—a departure from our previous experiences, which had been sleek and seamless. The reception area's decline was echoed throughout the hotel.

Within our spacious but dimly lit room, sad, tired vibes floated amidst the well-used furniture. Time had drained the drapes and carpeting of their original vibrant red color, but fiscal considerations precluded their replacement. The bathroom's pretty pink striped wallpaper was peeling in a few spots, and the tub emptied its watery load with all the speed of rush hour traffic on the Cross Bronx Expressway.

One of my first stops after unpacking was to go see Lenore, the tall strawberry-blonde owner of the hotel's elegant dress boutique that was situated in a green-carpeted arcade. She possessed a gift for choosing the right outfit to diminish or enhance (as the need might be) her customers' figures.

Besides great taste, Lenore had always exhibited a ready smile and a relaxed, friendly personality. On my last visit, she had presented me with a white silk flower.

"When you wear it, think of me," she had laughed.

Two petite brunette women greeted me as I entered the shop.

"Lenore passed away two years ago," they responded to my query with downcast eyes.

I had known that Lenore had been ill, but according to her, the chemo had seemed to be working . . . . Quickly I exited the store. My usually voracious appetite for shopping vanished like fireflies in an early country dawn.

The Asian garden, located just outside the glass-enclosed dining room approach, was still a source of beauty and tranquility. At night, the garden's dark green herbage and tinkling mini-pools were enhanced by pink, blue, and yellow spotlights. Unfortunately, on this visit, it was impossible to linger in admiration, because the air conditioning in that area, as well as in several other hallways and passages, had been cut back in a money-saving attempt. Previously, gazing at the glowing colors, I had seen a rainbow. Now, I could only experience an unwelcome blast of sweltering air.

I remembered a time when this very corridor had been filled with beautifully gowned, bejeweled and perfumed ladies on the arms of black-suited gentlemen. As they made their way into dinner, flashbulbs had constantly exploded, courtesy of the paparazzi-like hotel photographers.

The dining room itself still retained some of its former beauty. The red paisley and flowered carpet exactly matched the festoons draped on the high windows. Appetizing aromas filled the warm, thick air, along with the rattling of flatware and the clattering of utilitarian white dishes. However, the portions of food were smaller than those that I had remembered, and second helpings, once a given, were now obtained with difficulty from a reluctant kitchen.

Could it have been forty years ago when, in this same dining room, the table had been piled high with the famous Catskill breakfast? The salty smell of lox and whitefish had combined with the pungency of fried eggs and the sweet fragrance of syrupy French toast. It had been late

August, and the marigold-tinted sunlight streaming in already had an autumnal slant.

"Next week it will be September," a tall waitress had remarked, the forthcoming season's crispness foreshadowed in her precise tones.

Of course, fall did indeed arrive soon after, but now autumn also described the time of my life. The hands of the clock had moved with astonishing rapidity, and the hotel and I had both grown old, seemingly in the blink of an eye.

Our visit had been arranged to coincide with the holiday of *Shavuot*, a festival that commemorates the giving of the Ten Commandments and the *Torah* (law) to the Jewish people. Prayer services were held in the nightclub, which had been temporarily converted into a makeshift synagogue.

On other, non-religious occasions, this room's every show had commenced with a display of sweeping, swirling lights that inevitably evoked "oohs" and "ahs" from the delighted audience. The presentation's brilliance had been intensified by the midnight-blue walls, and the beauty of the light show managed, even for a moment, to obscure the realities of glaringly bright emergency rooms and tastefully appointed funeral chapels.

Throughout the holiday, the cantor's clear tones seemed to retroactively purify the club after the years of vulgar and profane jokes that had echoed against the now chipped and peeling interior.

The modestly dressed worshippers contrasted sharply with my memories of scantily clad revelers who had frequented this domain nightly, dancing with abandon to the band's brassy tones as they awaited "Showtime" with almost childlike anticipation.

The rhythm of our final day was disrupted by heavy rain—showers, booming thunder, and flashing lightning. Towards evening, the rain dissipated and I walked through damp, sweet-smelling grass to the small lake that dominated the rear of the hotel's grounds.

This small body of water had always been one of my favorite spots—surrounded by the sloping green hills of the golf course, flanked by tall fir trees and a once brightly colored gazebo that was now sun-bleached and in poor repair. The exact hour of my twenty-sixth birthday had been spent rowing on the lake's shallow depths and had been a moment of perfect contentment. I had been young enough to take for granted return trips to beloved locales, and naïve enough to believe that treasured experiences could always be relived.

Now, the sunset's mauve and orange reflections were laced on the dark teal water, between the thick green lily pads.

In the distance, thunder sounded.

THE SAXONY

"Nothing is forever."

As I age, I hear this phrase with increasing frequency from friends and acquaintances. It is usually delivered with a resigned shake of the head and a protracted sigh. Now the thought was more than just a philosophical observation. It had taken on a sad reality during my latest visit to Florida.

I had just learned that the last remaining kosher hotel in Miami Beach, the Saxony, had been sold. It would, most likely in the very near future, be demolished. The land where it had stood for over fifty years would now be far more valuable as a potential site for one of the high-rise condominiums that were increasingly springing up as a result of the current real estate boom.

Many other hotels had previously been beaten into oblivion by the wrecker's ball. But the Saxony? The Saxony?

Through the years, the hotel had lost many of its glamorous features—a glass elevator, elaborate antique lobby furnishings, fashionable stores—but it had also evolved into a *heimishe* (cozy) place, a comfortable if less than elegant home away from home.

The upscale South Beach hotels, several blocks away, featured sterile black and white glass and marble lobbies that seemed to exude an ambiance that somehow was disdainful of those who were not celebrities or billionaires. Their frigid interiors offered no place for a weary, perspiring walker to rest, even for just a moment.

In contrast, the Saxony was furnished with large, overstuffed green chairs and sofas. The hotel was renowned and appreciated as a welcoming oasis on a long, hot stretch of Collins Avenue. And people, many of them senior citizens and non-guests, did sit—to admire the "old is new again" ocher art deco columns with their lacy brass grille work, the tan marble floors and walls, as well as the huge, ornate crystal chandeliers.

The hotel's nightclub/synagogue, the Veranda Room, with its mural of antebellum southern life, echoed the lobby's filigree accents, although here they had been crafted in pristine white. The small stage with its polished wooden floor had been the setting for many excellent evening shows over the years—singers, musicians, and comedians. Even now, during the day, an elderly toupee-wearing entertainer with an electric keyboard sang thirties and forties hits ("Baby face, you've got the cutest little baby face") in a trembling voice to the delight of an enthusiastic senior audience. As the sky began to turn pink began in the late afternoon, his music also graced "Happy Hour," a time when free drinks were served to guests. The most popular beverage among the seniors, the joke went, was vodka laced with prune juice. The entertainer's serenade was a sort of musical last meal before the hotel's execution.

On Jewish holidays and the Sabbath, the room took on a more somber mood. Gone was the glaring show-time spotlight, now replaced by more subdued illumination. Many worshippers, some from the surrounding Collins Avenue condominiums, came to listen to the cantor's heartfelt, imploring tones and to join others in celebrating their ancient tradition. Prayer books of every description and age were piled high on large tables that had been placed in the rear of the room. The services' sweet conclusion, traditional receptions of sponge or marble cake and wine, was served in a nearby card room that had been temporarily expropriated for the collations.

Through the tall glass windows of the Veranda Room, an unobstructed view of the beach's beige sand and crashing white-capped waves could be admired. At night, the water's light-colored foam contrasted sharply with the blackness of the ocean below and the sky overhead.

Adjacent to the entertainment/worship space, the large dining room's own internal sea of white tablecloths rose above the green floral carpeting. Mornings, sunlight filtered in to brighten waiting glasses of orange juice that seemed to salute the new day. In the evening, palm trees were silhouetted against the red and orange sunset, and the air was heavy and warm with the appetizing odors of freshly prepared, delicious food.

The five elevators that transported vacationers to their rooms had been, for many years, the subject of jokes by veteran visitors—the "Saxony workout" was running for an elevator and yelling "Hold it!" at the same time. The conveyances' arrivals were heralded by heartily dinging bells alerting the waiting guests that they could now ascend to their quarters.

Upstairs, long narrow hallways with creaking floors led to unpretentious lodgings that were decorated with 1950s Italianate furniture. Front rooms faced Collins Avenue. They also commanded a view of teal green Indian Creek, large homes with terra cotta roof tiles, and the Miami skyline towering through the heat-induced haze.

However, most units featured small white-washed balconies that overlooked the amorphous turquoise pool, winding brown boardwalk, sun-splashed beach, and azure ocean. Relaxing on one of those terraces, fanned by gentle salty breezes, and being lulled by the sound of breaking surf had always seemed to be the ultimate in luxury. As I grew older, I reflected that if I was to die here, if my soul was to slowly float outward over the ocean and gently rise upon a cottony cloud, such a passing would be beautiful.

But now it was the Saxony that faced death and was inexorably becoming just another familiar, beloved refuge one couldn't return to, except in memory. The hotel's imminent closing signaled yet another sad life passage, an unwelcome reminder of the mortality that was intruding into a seaside paradise.

THE FLEA MARKET

When you die in Miami,
Your photos go in the garbage,
Your "things" are sent to the flea market.
Beige clocks with ebony numbers,
Golden, mirrored perfume trays
Pastel figurines of royalty,
Sparkling marcasite brooches,
Sensuous ruby velvet couches,
Your past,
Their future,
FOR SALE.